ADRENALINE CRUSH

ADRENALINE CRUSH

LAURIE BOYLE CROMPTON

MARGARET FERGUSON BOOKS | FARRAR STRAUS GIROUX | NEW YORK

Quotations on pages 3 and 173 from H. B. Paull's translation of
"The Steadfast Tin Soldier."

Excerpt on page 69 from INTO THE WILD by Jon Krakauer, copyright © 1996 by
Jon Krakauer. Used by permission of Villard Books, an imprint of The Random House
Publishing Group, a division of Random House LLC. All rights reserved.

Farrar Straus Giroux Books for Young Readers
175 Fifth Avenue, New York 10010

macteenbooks.com

Library of Congress Cataloging-in-Publication Data
Crompton, Laurie Boyle.
    Adrenaline crush / Laurie Boyle Crompton. — First edition.
        pages cm
    Summary: When seventeen-year-old Dyna, an avid thrill-seeker, falls and
shatters her leg, her life changes dramatically and she finds herself caught
between her boyfriend, who supports her newfound desire for safety, and a
young Iraq war veteran she meets at rehab who challenges her to take chances
again.
    ISBN 978-0-374-30061-6 (hardback)
    ISBN 978-0-374-30062-3 (e-book)
    [1. Wounds and injuries—Fiction.   2. Risk-taking (Psychology)—Fiction.
3. Adventure and adventurers—Fiction.   4. Love—Fiction.]   I. Title.

PZ7.C8803Adr 2014
[Fic]—dc23

2014016944

Farrar Straus Giroux Books for Young Readers may be purchased for business or
promotional use. For information on bulk purchases please contact Macmillan
Corporate and Premium Sales Department at (800) 221-7945 x5442 or by email
at specialmarkets@macmillan.com.

For Aidan: my little prince and laughing star

ADRENALINE
CRUSH

I

The soldiers were all exactly alike, excepting one, who had only one leg; he had been left to the last, and then there was not enough of the melted tin to finish him, so they made him to stand firmly on one leg, and this caused him to be very remarkable.

Hans Christian Andersen
"The Steadfast Tin Soldier"

My dark hair whips my bare back as I gain on the form cycling through the trees up ahead.

I may have just found my afternoon plaything. A perfect male specimen riding through the forest alone.

Exactly what I need.

Thrusting my shoulders over the handlebars of my mountain bike, I pedal faster. My tires gobble up the dirt trail as I close in.

My boy-toy-to-be turns his head and I get a glimpse of his profile under his helmet's visor. I recognize that face. Jay Something-or-other from school. My front tire wavers for just a breath.

Oh.

I had been hoping for some random boy to have fun with, but this is a boy from my class who is way too serious. Bordering on lame. Don't get me wrong, Jay's intelligent and I like a challenging conversation. But I'm not looking for a conversation today.

I'm looking for an afternoon fling.

Still.

I churn my strong legs back up to speed. He may not be the most exciting mark, but I'm trying to escape a nearly catatonic state of boredom. An hour ago I was lying on my deck, too hot to read the trail guide I'd laid over my face, when I heard a wasp chewing on the wood railing. The munching sound got louder and louder until I wanted to crawl out of my skin. I finally shouted, "Go chew on somebody else's damned deck!"

To a *wasp.*

Clearly, Dyna is ready to spend a little time with her own species.

"Heads up!" I stand on my pedals, lean over, and give two solid knuckle raps to Jay's helmet as I glide by.

Technically, I should be wearing one, too, but I ache for the wind. It's the reason I'm wearing just my bikini top and shorts and would probably ride naked if it wouldn't get me arrested. I glance back at a surprised-looking Jay, shift to a fast coast, and leave the next move in his hands.

Do you have the spirit of an adventurer hidden in there somewhere, Mr. Serious-bordering-on-lame?

I keep my eyes on the trail, but a smile spreads across my face as Jay catches up. *Okay, game on.* I change gears and pedal faster.

The trail we're on connects with the woods behind my house and runs sixteen miles to the north and south. I usually prefer spending time on it by myself, no matter what season it is.

Nature is most pure when experienced alone.

But I'm always up for a fun drive-by encounter with a boy when I'm bored.

I'm impressed Jay manages to match my pace and notice that his arms are actually quite muscular for a pale and overly serious type in a dorky bike helmet. "You're Dyna, right?" he pants.

"The one and mighty." I glance at his chin-strapped face. While he's not my type, he is probably what some girls consider swoon-worthy. His green eyes are rimmed with blond lashes, and even at this speed his straight teeth charm me when he smiles. I, personally, am not a swooner, and I don't really get girls who are, but I may have underestimated my afternoon plaything.

I'm glad.

I call to him, "It's so hot my tits are melting off!" Jay takes this as an invitation to turn his head and openly check out my rack.

"Still there," he confirms with a grin.

"Thanks for keeping an eye on them for me."

"Anytime." He's obviously not looking for a deep and meaningful relationship.

Good.

I just want to stir up this simmering July afternoon. And while fooling around is a definite possibility, I'm not about to hand over my pink. Past attempts have been made by a few bold boyfriend-types, but I'm keeping that territory unexplored until I find the right guy.

"What do you have planned for the summer?" he asks as I slow our pace.

"Hanging on the mountain." I look over at him. "Literally. *Hanging.* I've gone rock climbing almost every day since break started."

School finished nearly two weeks ago and I've been hooking up with a few random climbing buddies on the ridge. Our conversations basically consist of calling out things like *"On belay!"* *"Tension!"* and *"Climb on!"*

After a few pedals Jay says, "Yeah, I've been superbusy, too. Working on building my clips."

He interprets my silence as a desire for more details. "That's sort of like a portfolio for writers. I need them for my college applications."

"And here I figured you meant you'd been scrapbooking."

He laughs, and I turbo-blast down the trail. I'm nearly flying, but he speeds up and manages to keep less than a bike's length between us.

Now things are getting interesting.

I launch my bike over a protruding stone just as a striped caterpillar with a suicide wish inches into my pathway. Twisting my handlebars sharply, I avoid running the little guy through.

The caterpillar is spared, but my landing is shit and my back tire slides in the dirt.

My arms tense.

Frack! I struggle to keep from veering off the trail but plunge into a full-on skid.

A sour taste fills my mouth as I'm thrust toward a solid row of trees.

CrankinShitFrack! The wall of bark is coming at me fast. Leaning hard, I aim my bike so it's sliding sideways, tires first. I tense for impact.

In the background Jay shouts, "Ohmygod!"

Ignore him.

I grunt and dig in.

Pine needles and dirt form a violent cloud as I spin my wheels.

Come on, Dyna!

Powering through with everything I have, I finally grab traction. Regain control. I graze lumpy roots with my pedal, just clearing the tree.

Jay stops to process my near-blow, but I don't even slow down. My heart pumps pure adrenaline as I devour the trail. Tingles surge through my limbs. A rabbit makes way, and the air is filled with chirps and chatters.

I am the most alive thing in the woods right now.

I look back and toss a laugh to Jay. He lunges forward to catch up, but I keep my advantage all the way to the Wallkill River. When I reach the bridge I automatically rise, stand on my pedals, and let go of the handlebars. As I glide along the rumbling wooden planks I lock my knees, fling my arms open wide, and surrender to the river's vastness. The fresh air embraces me.

This is the only romance I'll ever need.

Jay speeds by me and my bike falters. *What the hell?* I grab my handlebars and he swings into a sideways stop, blocking my way.

My tires yelp against the brake pads. "What do you think you're doing?" I jump off my pedals onto the bridge's even planks.

"I could ask you the same thing." He reaches to steady my

bike and looks at me the way my parents might if they were the type to give stern parental glares. "You almost ate it back there."

"I'm fine. It was no big deal."

He laughs incredulously. "Are you always so wild? I mean, I heard you were a daredevil. You have a pretty epic reputation at school. But I didn't know you were semi-suicidal." His eyes are wide and the crease of concern in his forehead softens me. I wonder if he'll kiss me later.

"Don't worry, I'm not some psycho chick with a death wish. I've never even had a broken bone." Jay is gripping my bike so tight his knuckles look ready to pop. "Hey. Sorry if I scared you. It's just sort of my family's motto: Risk nothing. Do nothing. Die anyway."

Mom and Dad both have that saying tattooed on their shoulders in the form of a flying raven. My brother, Harley, rebelled and had his put on his rib cage, but I'm thinking the shoulder will work fine for me. I have a few other tats in mind, back of the neck, hip, inner wrist, but Dad's making me wait until I'm eighteen. He's pretty sure once I start with the ink I won't want to stop. He might be right.

Jay shakes his head, and I wonder if I should be looking for someone else to hang out with. *Someone who won't look at me this intensely.*

Finally, he moves his hand from my bike to my bare waist. His touch sends a tickling wave across my stomach, but it's probably just that human contact thing I've been lacking.

"Nice family motto. Can we try that 'Do nothing' part for the next hour or so while I catch my breath?"

I look down the bridge and see a couple lounging on one of the wooden benches in an intimate embrace.

"Sure," I say. "But not here. Let's go *do nothing* down by the swim hole."

"Swim hole?" Jay looks up and down the trail.

"Figures," I tease. "How long have you lived here? I'll show you." Veering around him I head off down the bridge and challenge, "But you've got to keep up, Scrapbook Junkie."

I glance back to see Jay leap onto his pedals. His straight teeth are set in a grimace as he flies past the stagnant couple and bears down on me.

I laugh with delight and speed up.

2

As we race down the path, Jay explains he doesn't usually ride the trail. He was on his way to the library to do some writing and spotted a flyer with a picture of a lost dog. The sign said the dog was last seen around here and he decided to take a detour to see if he could find it.

"So, you're telling me you went searching for some stranger's runaway dog? Like that's your job or something?"

Jay gives me a sheepish nod and I can't decide if this is the most ridiculous thing I've ever heard or the most adorable.

I make a sharp right turn onto the hidden path that leads to the swim hole and grind my bike to a halt. Jay stops, loops around impressively fast, and pedals after me again. The water isn't very far off the main trail, but it is well hidden.

"Did that sign back there say 'No Trespassing'?"

"Pshaw." I laugh. "Just the water company. They don't really mean it."

When we reach the swim hole Jay sucks in his breath. "Holy shite, I never knew this was here."

"Cool, huh?" I try to imagine the oasis as if seeing it for the first time and have to admit it is pretty picture-freaking-esque. The water reflects the sheer, towering rock face that closes the swim hole in along the back and one side. Trees leap at every imaginable angle and splotches of sunlight dance in their shadows. To our right the woods rise up sharply with a well-worn path that leads to an enormous moss-covered rock outcropping. The natural diving platform peers over the swim hole and butts up against the rock face about halfway up the sixty-foot cliff.

But the most unique part is the set of rusted railroad tracks that arch down from the top of one of the cliffs into the water. The rails have a crazy drowned-roller-coaster appearance that gives the surrounding beauty a perfect touch of amusement park quirkiness.

It's one of my favorite places, and points go to Jay for the reverent look on his face right now. At least he gets it.

He asks, "Was this some sort of rock quarry?" At my shrug he squints up to where the tracks jump off the top of the cliff. "There were a bunch of cement factories around here at one time. I'll bet the tracks carried mined rock up there to the kilns."

"Wow, that's nearly fascinating," I mock.

"The water must be supercold. Who knows how deep down it goes."

"It is really cold, but it only gets deep over to the right." I let my bike drop to the ground, kick off my shoes, and smoothly pull my shorts down, revealing my bikini bottoms. "You coming in?"

Jay's eyebrows jump in appreciation. We grin at each other as he takes off his helmet, hangs it on his bike handle, and lifts his shirt. He is pale as milky quartz, but he must own a Bowflex or something because, *Damn!*

I give a wink, turn, and break into a running start toward the swim hole. Aiming for the deep end, I skim the surface in a perfect dive. The icy water seeps into me. I stay submerged, running my hands along the slimy rocks as my lungs plead for air.

I resurface, anticipating Jay's dive, but he's still back by our bikes, emptying the pockets of his shorts into his helmet. I dip underwater again and swim to where the tracks are swallowed by deep blackness. Diving down, I explore until the pressure boxes my ears. Jay must be right about this being an old rock quarry. When I'm forced up for air he's taking pictures of the swim hole with his phone and starts typing something into it.

"You taking notes or jumping in?" I call.

He tosses his phone into his helmet and charges toward me, arms and legs pumping the air as he leaps into the water. I squeal appreciatively when he resurfaces beside me and splashes my face.

"Easy! I'm a delicate flower!" I grab on to his shoulders in a way that is not at all flora-like and pull him under.

He rises back up. "More like *wild*flower." Laughing, he grabs me by the waist and easily tosses me off to the side. Which is kind of cool since I was half trying to hang on to him and I'm pretty strong.

I sputter and cough when I resurface, and Jay is beside me asking, "You okay?"

"Always." I smile.

He leans back in the water. "This place is incredible."

"I know. You should write a poem about it."

"I'm a journalist, not a poet."

"That's a shame." I put my hand on his shoulder and lean in. "I'm really into poets."

He wraps an arm around me and his gaze deepens. "Well then, I may need to work on my iambic pentameter."

Arching my back, I look directly at his lips. His arm tenses up when I close my eyes. I move closer and . . .

"Psych!" I splash his face, break from the embrace, and swim gleefully toward shore.

"Dy-na!" He laughs.

Pulling myself out of the water, I pound my feet around the dirt trail toward the rock platform and scramble up the easy climbing-holds to the outcropping connected to the cliff. Jay is still treading water when I step forward onto the ledge about thirty feet above his head. The soft moss against my calloused soles makes me feel buoyant. I raise my hands above my head, mimicking a dive.

"Please tell me you're not serious," Jay calls up.

"Yeah, right." I'm still over the deep end of the swim hole, but I'm much too high up to dive without risking a broken neck on the surrounding rocks if my aim is off. And it just so happens I was telling the truth when I said I'm not some psycho chick with a death wish. I swing my arms back to build momentum and spring out, propelling myself over the water as far as I can get. I aim my feet for Jay, but he moves smoothly out of the way before I slice through the surface.

The water suspends me in its green coolness. I raise my arms over my head, open my eyes, and let my body go limp. Everything slows in this underwater world.

I want to stay here. Grow gills and extend this perfect summer moment forever. My hair floats gently as my mind etches every detail onto itself. The stillness. Jay's headless underwater body so white it glows. Light piercing the water from above, stroking the rocks with its bright fingers. My weightlessness as I'm drawn slowly upward.

I unfreeze my arms, but only to thrust them several times, pushing myself back down to the depths. Holding on a minute longer.

Finally, I float upward and smooth my hands over my wet hair as I emerge. If I was alone, I'd head back below. Instead, I look at Jay's grin.

"You really are wild," he says, and I want to reward him for seeing me. With a flourish so smooth it would make a mermaid gasp, I dart to him and wrap my hands around his shoulders. He keeps an amused look, waiting for the splash and tease as I draw closer. Water drips down his face. When I'm so close we're breathing each other's breath, his expression turns serious.

I resist the temptation to psych him out again and brush my lips lightly against his. Barely touching. He presses back with growing pressure. When our kiss deepens, his mouth is a few degrees cooler than mine and he tastes like spearmint. Nice. I pull back quickly and see naked desire in his eyes. Giddiness bubbles up over winning this game. I push off him and head back for dry ground.

This time he follows me to the edge. "Dyna—"

But when he stretches his Bowflex arms to pull himself out after me, I say, "No, wait here." He obeys, bobbing back in the water to his neck, and I rush up the trail along the side again.

"Are you almost done playing around?" he calls.

"Never!" I announce when I reach the mossy stage above. I disappear from his view, making my way through the pitch pine to the spot where the platform meets the wall of rock face.

"I am not rescuing you if you drown!"

"Fine!" I call back. "Bet I'm a better swimmer than you anyway!"

His laugh rises up on the weak breeze and I imagine I can smell his spearmint breath. I quickly analyze the rock face leading to the top where the tracks careen down from their crazy sloping angle. There are a few obvious holds, but it's a rough climb. I've never considered scaling it before.

"What the hell are you doing?" Jay sounds concerned and I want to keep him in suspense. Spotting a clear foothold, I place my bare toes into it. Luckily, my brother, Harley, got me started climbing barefoot, so mounting the side of this cliff feels almost as natural as riding my bike.

I dig my fingers into a small vertical crease and find a waist-high foothold that boosts me up quickly. I don't have a plan, but the rush keeps me moving upward. The moment I clear the bushes and Jay sees just how high I am he calls out, "Dyna!"

I turn my face toward the rough wall of rock so he can't see my smile and continue climbing. I'm good at spotting hand- and foothold combinations, and the climb energizes me now that I'm in it. It's easier than it probably looks from below, but the higher I get the more my progress slows. Securing my foot into a deep crevice, I stop and rest my arms for a moment while I even out my breathing. Looking down, I realize I'm more than halfway between the platform and the top. I scan the cliff face above and spot a handhold that sits a challenging distance from my reach.

Jay tries a lighter tone. "Come on down, the water's fine."

With a grunt, I swing my arm, extend my spine, and inch my fingers into the hold. I continue pressing upward hold by hold. Some are easier than others. It's the demanding ones that have me captivated.

I realize I've turned on my "porn star sound track." My climbing buddies love to tease me about the groans I make as a climb gets difficult, and right now I'm building toward a moaning climax. I feel strong, and within five well-placed moves I can see the top. High on my accomplishment, I look down at Jay, and my eye catches a thin fracture line leading to my left foothold.

My stomach plummets and I quickly examine the surrounding rock face for other signs of choss.

"You are seriously freaking me out!" Jay yells up.

"I'm great." I stay focused, tapping the rock with my palms and listening for hollow places to avoid as I climb on.

My heart pumps endorphins through my system, and by the time I haul myself over the top I'm levitating. Every inch of me is free. I lie on my back and close my eyes, running my throbbing palms against stiff blades of grass.

I feel incredible.

If I could somehow capture this feeling right now,
bottle it up,
I'd share it with the world and there would be
no more war,
no famine,
no people hating other people.
Just life and love.

I open my eyes.

And this beautiful wide blue sky
connecting us all.

"You okay?" Jay's voice floats up.

I roll onto my stomach and peer down over the edge. "Never better."

Jay has climbed out of the water and is dripping a wet trail back and forth along the shore. "How the hell are you getting down, Dyna?"

I'm not exactly sure of my answer to that. Sitting up, I mull over my options. I didn't like the look of that fissure, so rather than go back the same way, I decide to walk along the edge looking for an easier route down. But then I have the best idea ever.

Scooting around to the other side where the rusty iron rails plummet off the cliff, I grab the first wooden tie and try to shake the track. As I expected, it doesn't budge. Satisfied, I place my hands on the uneven plank and shout, "Heads up!"

Jay puts his palms to his eyes. "Please don't do that." Sliding his hands to the sides of his head, he groans and repeats, "I am not going to rescue you!"

"You won't need to." I shine my brightest smile down on him. He raises his hands up in the air as if he can keep me safe from where he's standing.

I peer over the edge and my mind resists my plan as it takes in the way the tracks arc out and down, with every fourth or fifth tie missing. This side of the swim hole is much more shallow and the rocks gnash their teeth at me just below the water's surface. My lungs spasm at the steepness of the drop as I crawl out onto the level tracks on my hands and knees. *Come on, Dyna, this will be easy*. I move forward slowly, and the distance to the ground makes every second clear and sharp and real.

"You're crazy!"

"Trying to focus here."

Using the rough wooden ties to support my hands and knees, I travel farther out over the water. Now that I've started, it's easy to keep moving.

When I reach the section where the rails dip steeply, I realize I need to turn my body completely around. If I can get my feet in front of me and flip over, I can climb down as if the tracks were nothing more than an oversized ladder.

This is a simple enough move; it's the mental part that makes me pause. The rocks continue taunting me from an impossible distance below, and I wish I'd thought this through a little better.

"Please, dear God, be careful." Jay is starting to get on my nerves.

"God has got nothing to do with this," I call down in a warning tone. He's back to treading water at the bottom of the tracks, and I feel bad for getting annoyed at him.

Placing my left hand on the rusty rail beside me, I immediately recoil from the skillet-hot iron and shake the sting off my palm.

"Are you okay?"

I hold up my reddened hand. "I'll live." Careful not to touch the fiery rails again, I rise from crawling to a kneeling position, put my arms in the air, and call "Wheeee!" as if I'm about to ride all the way down to Jay's waiting arms. He shakes his head.

I grasp the wooden tie behind my hips and slide one leg

forward so it's pointed out in front of me. Leaning to my left, I swing my other leg to join it and drop my butt squarely on the soft wood. I take a breath and prepare to turn over so I can climb down feetfirst.

Looking at Jay's intense expression, I can't resist giving him a sexy one-shoulder smile. He cracks a grin of defeat and starts climbing up the rails toward me, presumably to rescue me now that I'm fine. *I can let him play hero,* I decide with a chuckle.

The wooden tie I'm sitting on dips to the right and my chuckle chokes into a gasp.

It's as if the sleepy roller coaster has sprung to life.

Jay's eyes bulge as he starts lunging up the tracks toward me.

The rotten board lets out a groan

and I'm helpless as I'm

pitched forward.

No! No! No!

And the stupid

useless

rotted chunk

of wood breaks free in three jarring stages.

I'm vaguely aware of Jay yelling instructions

but there is nothing to be done.

Gravity is greedy and the momentum is too much.

I claw for the rails. Clutch the sear of iron. But my grasp doesn't even slow my drop and everything I'm trying to hang on to rises up out of my reach. I am

falling.

Fast and hard and toward

rocks and water that's too shallow
to catch me.
To save me.

I usually love falling. Bungee jumping. Parasailing. Even riding the rickety parachute ride at the Ulster County Fair. I've
never been falling like this.

I'm flailing and
lost and
glimpse a blur of
Jay diving back into the water that
rushes at me too fast too fast too fast and then everywhere—
black.

3

Sirens batter me awake. I'm lying on my back getting jostled by a rockslide that won't settle.

A hand is cradling mine.

"Dyna?"

I want to tell whoever is controlling the rockslide to knock it the hell off and let me sleep already.

"Come on, Dyna."

Memory and reality collide and I know I'm riding in the back of an ambulance.

Pain gnaws at the edges of my consciousness and my right leg feels like it may have been chopped off with a dull ax.

Everything is different.

I want to curl into a cocoon. Get away from the rockslide that is still happening. To be held still and safe. I'm so tired. *Pull it together, Dyna,* I command, gathering feeble wisps of determination.

"Dyna. Please."

I open my eyes to a close-up view of Jay. His wet hair is slicked back and he is staring at my face as if the two of us have known each other all our lives. Like I mean something to him.

We're suspended in each other's gaze for a wide-open moment but then
the thing
that thing
that happened
to me
that landed us together
is here.
I blink against the images rushing through my mind—
sky-and-water-and-the-black.
I shut my eyes.
Despite the jostling, Jay is gentle when he strokes the side of
my face. He squeezes my hand and I wince. "Sorry," he says.
"You must have burned your palm on the rail." But neither one
of us lets go.
I fight heavy eyelids, forcing myself to look at him. I see he has
a tiny scar on his cheek, right where the skin dimples in when
he purses his lips.
Ignoring the pain rising from my leg, I say, "Thought you
said you wouldn't rescue me." My voice sounds strange. Weak.
Jay snorts and shakes his head back and forth slowly. "I
thought you said I wouldn't need to."
I close my eyes again and concede, "I guess you've got me
there."
"That's right." Jay's voice soothes against my ear. "I've got
you."
I slip back to the black.

When I claw my way out again, I'm used up and the world has turned minty white.

Thankfully, I'm out of the rockslide, but Jay is gone. My right leg now feels as if it's been run through a wood chipper, and I'm lying on a bed being rolled down a wide corridor. Crinkled white ceiling tiles and fluorescent lights alternate endlessly above me.

I try to sit up, but my head is too massive to raise more than a few inches. I sink back down to a pillow that crunches as if it's filled with wadded paper. "Jay . . . ?" I say, but my voice trails off and my fight to remain conscious drains away. A hovering masked chin dips down saying . . . something. The muffled voice is kind, but I'm too far away now to make sense of what it's telling me.

Quiet and stillness have finally descended and my leg feels like it's being dragged toward the ceiling. The whole right side of my body throbs. When I open my eyes my mother's there. She's holding my hand and looking at me as if she hasn't seen me in weeks. Dad stands behind her, hands on her shoulders. When I blink at him his face crumbles in on itself for a flash.

"Welcome back, Dyna Glider," he says.

I haven't been so happy to see my parents since I was a little kid.

Despite the fact that I'm lying down, my head feels spinny. I breathe in disinfectant, and it's oddly comforting. My right ankle hurts bad, but I'm able to separate from most of the pain and push it away.

A petite nurse gives me a lipsticked grimace as she works her way around my bed. She reminds me of a nervous field mouse as she checks the plastic bags of fluid going into and coming out of me. When Dad moves his arm so she can get by him, she practically leaps out of her pink crocs.

Typical.

When I look at my folks, I see Mom, who can sew anything imaginable without following a pattern and who makes detailed charcoal sketches of plants and insects in order to relax. And I see Dad, whose big bushy eyebrows bump together when he's being serious, which is most of the time, but who has the loudest booming laugh that reverberates for miles and makes it totally worth the effort to coax it out of him. I see my parents and I'm overwhelmed with love for them, but I know that's not what this nurse sees.

This nurse sees Mom's chunks of purple highlights and her sundress with no bra. She sees Dad's hair snaking down his back in a long row of elastic hair ties.

And especially—I guarantee this—she sees the tattoos.

Both of my parents are completely covered in ink. Dad's tattoos include many styles from various artists over the years, but he's the best tattooist north of Manhattan and he's done all of Mom's inkwork. He calls her body his masterpiece. She's gorgeous and gets stopped on the street all the time by folks who want to snap her picture.

I look over at the kaleidoscope design that starts at her shoulder and wraps down around a baby's handprint on her elbow. My handprint. Growing up with the mosaic of familiar images and knowing the meaning behind the art, I absolutely love the way my parents look. But I've learned that lots of people have trouble seeing past a person's skin.

The nurse busies herself making scribbles on a clipboard before scampering away around the empty bed beside me and out the door.

"How're you feeling, honey?" Mom asks. She strokes my hair as if I'm an angel that only she can see. My accident seems to have brought out some supernurturing mother alter ego she's been repressing.

It's kind of creeping me out.

"Hard to believe." Dad rubs his hands together. "Made it all the way to seventeen without needing a hospital. That's a good run, sweetheart."

Everything's too heavy; even the air weighs on me. Twinges of pain run along my shin and—I'm hit with a horrible thought. I whisper, "Will I be able to climb again?"

"Well," Mom says. "I mean . . ." She smooths my blanket. "You'll need . . . physical therapy . . ." Bile fills the back of my throat as my mother falters for words. She never falters for words.

"What your mom is trying to say," Dad cuts in, "is that your leg got pretty beat up in your fall."

Mom's voice is soft. "The way you landed on the . . . rocks splintered your . . . ankle. But hey—" She rubs my arm. "It could've been much worse." Her voice catches.

I look at Dad. "You were knocked unconscious by the trauma of your fall. If you'd been alone you might have drowned."

"It was a good thing that boy was there." Mom gives me a

weak smile. "He saved you." I picture Jay carrying me out of the water all broken and bleeding.

"The doc had to go a little medieval on that ankle, Glider," Dad jokes, but his eyebrows stay fused together. "Pins and screws and clamps. But they got you pieced back together all right."

"The operation went well." Mom nods. "The doctor said he was pleased."

"Now they just have to watch you for infection. It was an open break and the way your bones were exposed . . . there's a chance . . ." Dad doesn't go on.

"A chance of what?" I clutch the sides of the bed. "A chance I could lose my foot?"

I feel helplessly trapped in a way I hadn't a moment ago.

"Easy there," he says. "They think they got everything cleaned out and they're pumping you full of antibiotics right now, but it's too early to tell."

"Visualize healing," Mom says soulfully. "Believe for zero infection."

Dad looks me in the eye. "Depending on how much mobility you get back, there's also a chance you might need a cane . . . permanently." His face crumbles again for a flash and I look away.

Please-no-please-no-please-no.

Out loud I say, "This isn't happening."

"You're okay," Mom says, as if she's the one who needs to hear it. "Everything is okay."

I take a deep breath and try to believe the words of this calm, meditative woman who is posing as my mother.

Everything is okay.

"That there is some fucked-up shit!" My big brother walks in the door and raises his pierced eyebrow at me.

"Har-ley," Mom chides. "Language, please." Which isn't really fair since she swears plenty when she thinks we can't hear her. And sometimes when she knows we can.

"Nice work, sis," Harley says, as he hands Dad a sweating bottle of water. "I've broken my ankle but never had my tib rip through the skin before. You'll have a gnarly shin scar and serious bragging rights." He looks proud of me. "Classic Dynamite."

I wince as a throbbing pain shoots up my leg.

Mom reads my expression. "The doctor mentioned your meds would be wearing off soon." Dad starts tapping at the call button.

"Let's try to get you some of the good stuff," he says, and winks at me as Nurse Nervous pokes her head into my room.

"She's in terrible pain," my mother says.

The nurse lifts my chart off the foot of the bed. Dad smiles and tells her, "You're going to want to give her something extra-strong. There's a high tolerance in our genes."

She looks at the tattoo sleeves covering Dad's arms and squeaks, "She can have more Percocet in another half hour."

Harley whispers under his breath, "Mmmm, I got Percocet for my busted clavicle."

Dad says, "Thank you, ma'am," as the nurse heads toward the door. He always treats the folks who don't see past his tattoos just as nice as can be. He calls it "pardoning the ignorant."

My mother, on the other hand, is not so forgiving. "Thirty minutes," she says sharply, and the nurse scurries her final steps away from us.

"You're lucky," says Harley, and we all look at him. Gesturing to the empty bed he clarifies, "No roommate. Last time I was here overnight I had a guy with night terrors."

I look at Dad. "Take me home?"

" 'Fraid not, Dyna Glider."

Mom offers, "I'll stay with you. I can sing you to sleep like I did when you were little." With that, she launches into a falsetto chorus of "Blackbird."

"Seriously?" I look at Dad. "Please get her out of here, she's starting to freak me out."

"Let's go, Beth." He moves to pull Mom up by her shoulders. "Once they give her more pain meds she's just going to pass out anyway." He lifts her hand-stitched satchel over her kaleidoscope shoulder. It's one of the bags she sews for the Groovy Blueberry clothing store in town. She gives my face an embarrassing number of wispy kisses before Dad is able to guide her away from my bed.

"You get some rest," he says. "We'll see you tomorrow."

Harley gives me a wink and leans in. "Enjoy the high, sis."

"Thanks, freak." I smile as he lopes after our parents. I've been looking forward to the kick-ass birthday gift he promised when I finally turn eighteen in September. Skydiving. When he isn't working one of the registers at the Park-n-Shop, he spends his time at a nearby parachuting mecca called the Ranch, and now that he's hit five hundred dives he's qualified to do tandem jumps. Apparently the only thing more awesome than jumping out of a plane is strapping another human being to your chest and *then* jumping out of a plane. I'll finally be old enough to jump with him. I imagine stepping into the sky. Falling.

My lingering smile turns stale.

The hospital room is quiet without my loud family, and I realize I forgot to ask them if they got to meet Jay. I glance at the raised appendage that is my damaged leg and try to ignore the chains of regret pulling at me. But my mind wants to dig through the rubbish of the day and figure out how I ended up here. What did—? And I realize:

I chose this.

The thought hits me so hard I rub my forehead.

Everything—the fall, nearly dying, the possibility of being permanently crippled. These must be the experiences I've been searching for. The logical extreme conclusion to all my risk taking. I simply reached the end of the road I've been traveling down full-speed for years. Did I really chase after this with everything I have?

Maybe I *am* one of those psycho chicks with a death wish after all.

4

"Stop torturing yourself." Mom snatches *Rock with a View* from my hands.

"Hey," I say, even though I know she's right. Scanning through my well-worn trail guide, picturing each path, is only making things harder.

The orange living room couch has effectively become my prison for the past week since my accident. I'm shackled in place by my elevated ankle, and my summer activities have been reduced to lying flat on my back doing nothing.

Even sleep has become a rare escape as I spend nights here endlessly repositioning. The stairs might as well be blocked by a barbed wire fence. I glance over at them now, mocking me with their even, gentle rise, and I marvel at how far I've fallen. It seems I've dodged the bullet of infection, so at least I get to keep my mangled ankle and foot, but it's still way too soon to tell just how useful they will be.

If there's too much tissue damage I could still be a candidate for fusion, which means they'd lock my ankle at a ninety-degree angle so I could lead a normal life free from excruciating pain.

And free from rock climbing. And free from— I cut myself off and stare at the plaster ceiling as some TV nature show about insects drones on in the background.

"Is Jay coming by today?" Mom asks.

I nod and pull out my smile. Jay's daily visits are the only bright spot in this festering cesspool of suckage that my life has become. A wave of pain inches up my shin, and I breathe through my teeth until it fades to a bearable level. I stopped taking my pain pills after a few days because at least the sharp pangs give me something to focus on.

The sun tauntingly soaks the outdoors as the narrator on television describes the intricate communal structure of an ant colony. *The ceiling is definitely lower than it was yesterday.*

Just as my mind is about to snap with restlessness I hear a familiar car pull up.

When Mom opens the door, Jay's face is partially hidden by a huge mass of wildflowers.

"How's the patient doing?" He crosses the living room to my couch holding out the bright bouquet.

"They're beautiful, Jay," I say. "But the ones from the other day are still alive."

"Never too many wildflowers for you."

"What a perfect tiger lily for sketching." Mom admires an orange blossom. "Let me get these in water."

Jay hands them to her and holds up a paperback copy of a book he told me about called *Into the Wild.*

Mom leans over to read the title. "Now why on earth would you give her a book like that?"

"Don't worry," Jay says. "It definitely qualifies as a cautionary tale. Shows just how dangerous nature can be if it's not respected."

Satisfied, Mom heads for the kitchen with my flowers, and I try to sit up.

"Whoa, remember, toes above the nose," Jay says.

I lie back but reach my arms up for him. He kneels down beside me and with a look of tenderness he kisses me. We linger a moment and I feel his lips pull up into a grin.

"Jay, is that your Subaru in the driveway?" Dad's voice thunders in the doorway.

Jay is practically a blur as he shoots up and spins around to face my father. "Sorry. If you need me to move it I can."

Dad eyes him. He's been very nice to Jay the couple of times they've met, but I'm afraid walking in on us kissing may have just changed that. Drastically. When it comes to guys trying to date me, Dad considers it his job to "weed out the weak."

Sure enough, Dad pretends to scratch his shoulder, clearly displaying my name tattooed in big letters down his forearm. Moving into Jay's personal space he asks, "Do you know how precious my daughter is to me, Jay?" Dad flicks his fist, making my name pop slightly, and prods, "Well, do you?"

Judging by the look on Jay's face, he just felt a little pee come out.

"You can park your chick car on the *left* side of the driveway," Dad commands, and Jay mumbles something about having to go home anyway.

He gives Mom and me hurried goodbyes, and as soon as he's outside I scold my father for being so harsh.

Dad chuckles. "I'm just doing my fatherly duty."

"You enjoyed that too much," I accuse. "Isn't it enough that Jay saved my life?"

Dad's expression softens as he glances at my foot propped up on pillows. "That's the only reason I didn't toss him out on his ass as soon as I saw him kissing you, Dyna. This guy seems way too white-bread for my girl."

"He's been very good for her." Mom walks back in and places the fragrant wildflowers on the side table near my head.

I listen to Jay's car pull away and go back to watching the smooth blank ceiling. Allowing my eyes to unfocus, I try not to think about how unbearable things will become if Dad just chased him away for good.

That boy is the only perk this prison has.

"I'm right behind you," Jay says. It's two weeks later and we're finally back on the trail that runs behind my house. But instead of soaring on my bike, I'm hobbling along on my crutches. My ankle is being compressed and held in place by a huge plastic contraption that comes up to my knee. It's secured with thick seat belt–like straps that might as well be around my neck the way the stupid thing is suffocating me. It's called an air cast, but we've nicknamed it Frankenfoot.

I'm trying to be grateful for the fact that I am no longer horizontal.

Jay puts his hand on my shoulder. "Do you need to rest?"

Despite conquering the simple staircase, I'm still sleep-deprived.

Now I just lie awake in my own bed staring at the ceiling, but I don't need to rest at the moment. What I need is for Jay to kiss me. I hop to the edge of the trail, put my crutches together, and lean my back carefully against the wide trunk of a tree. Settled, I let my crutches drop with a clatter and give Jay a look that says "Come here."

With a smirk he moves in front of me, stroking the side of my face with the backs of his fingers. He seems to have gotten taller since the day of my accident.

"You okay?" He moves his arm down to my waist and I will him to kiss me.

He leans forward,

tilts his head in that beautiful way,

and draws me in like a breath.

The familiar hint of cool spearmint is there and I'm lost in the sweetness of it.

It's as if I knocked on Jay's bike helmet that day and he answered by saving me. I've been landing in his arms in every way since.

He groans and pulls back, but the longing in his eyes remains. Reaching for him, I wrap my arms around his shoulders. Effortlessly, and taking care not to bump Frankenfoot, he lifts me up to himself. I'm floating, weightless, and slide my hands to the sides of his face.

We press our lips together again. He settles into the kiss, leans back, and I'm

thrown off-balance.

Drop my

hands back down to his

shoulders. Hang on. "Eeep."

But he has me all along. He raises his chin and I watch the longing in his eyes drain as his expression shifts to something else. Worry.

"Sorry." He sheepishly places me back on the ground. Holds me steady with one hand while he retrieves my crutches. His tenderness is touching but I wasn't finished with that kiss. He helps me get situated with my crutches before guiding me down the trail.

Frustrated, I want to tell him I'm not feeble. I'm still Dyna. The one and mighty.

To show him, I lurch along the path, picking up speed until he has to lengthen his stride to keep up. The hint of a breeze brushes my face and loosens Frankenfoot's hold on my throat.

"Dy-na," Jay warns, and I turn my focus back to the ground so I don't fall.

But I continue moving faster and faster until I'm taking two hops on my good leg before literally launching myself along with the crutches. I'm actually starting to get a little distance.

"Dyna! What're you doing?"

I laugh back over my shoulder, but Jay's look of horror slows me down. I stop the launching action.

What is the matter with me?

Jay catches up and puts a hand on my shoulder until I come to a complete stop. "You need to be more careful." His voice is firm. "You don't want to make things worse by falling."

He's right, of course. I need to stop acting wild.

To change.

Long days on couch lockdown convinced me of that.

"Ready to head back?" Jay asks, even though it feels like we just got started. "It seems too soon to be pushing yourself so hard." I swear he'd be fine carrying me the whole way along the path.

I sink into my crutches. "I guess I should rest up for tomorrow."

"Where is this miraculous therapy place anyway? Can I drive you?"

I shake my head. "It's on the other side of the Gunks. Mom has this whole plan for us to *bond* over breakfast at the Village Tearoom."

"You two don't exactly strike me as the fancy-scones-and-pastries type."

"We're not," I say. "Not to mention we have to leave the house at eight-thirty to have time to sit around drinking designer tea before my session at ten. And Mom is *not* a morning person. She's been on this treasure-every-moment-together kick since my . . ." I don't say it. "Did I tell you she anointed me with the smoke of burning sage while I was trying to eat my lunch yesterday?"

Jay laughs. "That's awesome."

"I can hardly wait to find out what sort of nutty place she picked out for my therapy. I just wish she'd go back to normal." I look at him. "Well, I mean normal for *her*, anyway."

Jay says, "I don't think there's such a thing as normal after almost losing a child." My hands tighten on my crutches and he rubs my shoulder gently. "Let's go back to your house and hang out a little while before, uh, I have to go home and get my workout in." It turns out I wasn't so far off with my Bowflex theory. Jay has a gym set up in his basement where he spends time every day.

I look up into his face. "And this has nothing to do with the fact that my father gets home soon?"

"No," Jay says in an exaggerated way while nodding his head up and down. We laugh, and I tap his butt playfully with my crutch. He lunges to steady me before I can lose my balance and then he helps me reposition my crutches toward home.

Jay claims there's an ancient tradition that says since he saved my life he's now responsible for it.

He takes responsibility very seriously.

5

Mom won't go over the speed limit even though the stupid tea and scones took too long and we're running a full ten minutes late. An impatient car shadows us through the forest. Mom used to be the impatient one, flying down these winding roads, but even her driving has changed since my fall. Finally the car roars by as she turns off at a hanging wooden sign in the shape of a butterfly.

"Ulysses Inner Outer Healing Center," it reads in iridescent blue letters.

As we pull up the long driveway to the parking lot, an A-frame log cabin appears through the trees and I see a small group of people sitting on the deck overhead. None of them seem to be participating in any form of physical activity.

This is starting to look like a touchy-feely talk-about-our-emotions type setup. And crippling accident or not, I will never be a touchy-feely kind of girl.

"Um, where did you find this place?"

"Oh, you know." Mom gestures as if the house just fell out of the sky and landed in front of us. "I saw an article in the

Mid-Hudson Mantra. The Ulysses Center goes much deeper than traditional physical therapy. They specialize in highly traumatic cases and use a completely unique approach to holistic healing."

And . . . there it is.

"I had to beg them to fit you into this session. Actually started crying over the phone." At my look she adds, "I wasn't being manipulative. I was genuinely upset at the time."

I don't want to get out of the car, but I picture Mom crying on the phone to get me into this place where she believes they can help me. *I can do this.*

We make our way slowly up the stairs to the deck. By "slowly" I mean we're now fifteen minutes late and by "make our way" I mean I'm using both crutches positioned under one arm as I hang on to the railing with my other hand and hop up the stairs. Mom follows, holding out her arms on either side of me as if she is capable of catching me if I fall.

Steps leading up to a physical therapy group. What a fantastic idea.

When we reach the top I'm surprised to spot the distant purple outline of the Catskill Mountains through the tree branches. If they clear-cut this front yard they'd have an amazing view. Instead, the deck is surrounded by mature oaks and maples. A huge windowed wall runs along the back of the deck with a sliding door that leads into the building. Bird feeders dot the branches and a squirrel is hanging by his feet quickly emptying one of them. I smile. It's actually pretty nice up here.

I look around the circle of wooden Adirondack chairs. The people sitting in them remind me of when Mom experiments with fabric—combining various scraps until the results are so "out there" she ends up tossing it.

A patchwork quilt of busted-up folks.

Frankenfoot gives a moan. *Guess I'm in the right place.*

"You're late," a large shemale at the head of the circle snaps. His/her hair is short and curly and I take a moment, trying to determine gender. I check hands, wonder some more, and finally scan the neck for an Adam's apple. *Definitely female.*

"Say hello," she commands.

"Um, hi," I address the four others. "I'm Dyna and this is my mother?"

"Hello, Dyna. Goodbye, Dyna's mother," the woman says gruffly. "She'll be done at one o'clock sharp."

I give Mom a look that says, "Please don't leave me alone with these people," but she just hugs me before heading back down the steps. When she glances over her shoulder, I swallow at the worry on her face. Smiling bravely, I face the group.

A round-faced man sitting close by gives me a boyish smile and his blond hair falls into his eyes. When he raises his hand to wave at me, I notice his other forearm ends in an unexpected stump. I'm stunned as I return his wave, waggling my fingers, and then feel guilty for that. Like, "Looky over here. I've got fingers." *What is wrong with me?*

I'm not ready to be around other people.

The only empty chair is next to the blond guy, and it's so low to the ground there's no way to smoothly slide into it. I lean my crutches behind it, and after a few clumsy attempts I finally manage to drop my butt down hard. Leaning back makes me feel too vulnerable, so I hunch forward and look around the circle.

An older woman with gray hair twisted into two braids gives me a smile. She looks completely healthy and I wonder if she maybe wandered up here because she had nothing better to do this morning.

Beside her is a stunning Asian girl with a patch over one eye who appears to be in her early twenties. Her posture is rigid and her gaze takes me in with enough intensity for six eyes.

Next to her sits a black man with snaking scars running down both his arms. I'm pricked with sorrow for whatever happened to him, and I regret making these people wait for me.

The burly leader introduces herself as Miss Brauhn and tells me to call her Miss, which is a little funny since there is nothing Miss-like about her. Not that I'd consider laughing.

With a pointed look at me she says, "*As I was saying* . . . this is *inner* therapy. My sister takes care of the *outer* therapy in the wellness center." She points her thumb toward the sliding glass doors. The sun is shining too brightly against the glass for me to be able to see inside, but I can hear weights ringing out at even intervals. I try to envision her even burlier sister, but cannot.

"We will now go around the circle," Miss says gruffly. "You will introduce yourself and explain what happened to bring you here. Also, you're each to give a one-word description of yourself. I want you to think hard about who you are right now, today. Find your one word. Feel it. And then share your word with the group."

She nods for me to go first. *Great.*

"Hi. I'm Dyna. Named after the Harley Davidson line of Dyna Cycles." I'm greeted with warm smiles I didn't expect. "My ankle got really messed up when I was rock climbing. I took a bad fall at the old swim hole down in the valley? I guess it's actually an abandoned rock quarry." I swallow, hating the way my voice sounds.

"Anyway, the accident happened at the beginning of the month and the doctors say I should be able to switch from the crutches to a cane in a couple more weeks." I shrug. "Then I'm really hoping I'll be able to ditch the cane one day, too."

"And your one-word description?" Miss prods.

"Oh, um, I guess . . . just . . . fine."

"Fine?"

"Yes, like, I'm going to be fine." Miss nods knowingly, and I get annoyed when she starts to write on her pad. "I mean, I'll be okay," I tell her.

"Now your word is 'okay'?" she challenges.

I nod and curl my hands into my lap. I dropped from "the one and mighty" to "fine" and "okay" with one bad climb. I picture Jay and straighten my shoulders. Things could've been much worse. There is nothing wrong with being "okay."

The gray-haired lady introduces herself as Rita and explains that she broke her shoulder and collarbone a year ago when she fell during a cross-country skiing expedition. She points to a scar running down her upper arm and explains she's repeating a session here at Ulysses in order to get back full use. She flips a braid behind her back and churns her arm in a way that is actually pretty darn agile for someone her age. "See," she says, "I can't quite make it all the way around." In spite of her incomplete shoulder rotation, Rita's one-word description is "blessed."

"Hi, I'm Frank." The blond guy salutes us with his stump and then quickly tucks it back into his lap. "As you can see, I lost my left hand." He chuckles. "Sucks for me, I used to be a lefty." Nobody works up a laugh in return. "Really, I'm doing okay. Was my own fault, to be honest. Texting while driving."

His blond hair flops as he nods. "I was sending a 'That's what she said' to my buddy and the next thing I knew my delivery truck was rolling down an embankment. It crushed my wrist." He rubs his stump. "Turns out, FedEx gets pretty pissed when you total one of their trucks. I already had a few warnings for messing up: bent packages, late deliveries, that sort of thing, but this was a whole new level of damaged merchandise." Frank grins. "I guess my word for the day is 'unemployed.' But at least I'm the only one who got hurt by my stupidity."

"You think you feel stupid?" the scarred black guy says. "I got messed up because I was out hiking on a mountain during a lightning storm."

"You were struck by lightning?" I burst out, and a harmony of "ohs" spreads through the circle.

"Yeah, well, the storm came on kind of sudden. I figured it would pass by quick. In fact, when I got struck I was still on my way *up* the mountain."

I feel an instant connection with this young man as he rubs his arms. In his scars I see another bad experience I've been chasing after. I've certainly been out hiking during thunderstorms. I picture my parents crying in the hospital and swear I'll never climb a mountain in a storm again.

"The lightning trashed my nervous system and my arms are in constant pain. It's already kept me from planting season." He tells us he had to hire someone to take over the work on his small organic farm this summer.

Lightning guy tells us his name is Sam and his word is "Sparky" because that's what his friends have been calling him since he was struck. Miss pipes in. "Sparky it is then! A new nickname is a great way to acknowledge and embrace the impact your injury has had on your life."

"Excuse me, Miss," says the Asian girl. "I'm impressed with your reputation and success rate, but I'd rather not embrace any part of this." She points to her eye patch.

I nod my agreement.

"Here at Ulysses Inner Outer Healing Center we believe in something called the Struggle Factor. I want to share a little story." Miss leans forward. "There was once a young girl who happened upon a butterfly just as it was breaking out of its cocoon. The girl felt compassion for the butterfly struggling to get free, so she helped it along. Once freed, the butterfly slowly stretched its beautiful blue wings back and forth."

Miss looks meaningfully around the circle. "When the young girl's father came to fetch her for lunch she explained that she'd just helped the butterfly and was waiting for it to fly away. The father told her, 'I'm sorry, but that butterfly will never fly.'" Miss pauses for dramatic effect. "He told her, 'It is the struggle to free itself from the cocoon that strengthens the butterfly for flight.' Her attempt to help the butterfly had, in fact, doomed it to die."

With that, Miss lifts a large glass pendant from her broad chest. A blue butterfly is sealed inside. "That young girl was me," she says. "My father had the butterfly preserved and it now represents the struggle that each and every one of you must endure in order to free yourselves." She holds the bright pendant up high and announces dramatically, "It's a Ulysses butterfly. I've named the center after it."

"I suppose that explains the lack of a handicap ramp," I say half to myself, half to Frank. He gives a short laugh and Miss seems about to say something when her attention is drawn to a young man quietly limping up the stairs.

As he rises into view, the first thing I notice is the way his light blue eyes flash from his otherwise dark features.

He struggles a bit with the steps, but his determination makes pity impossible. Not that I'm in a position to pity him anyway. I had a hard time getting up them myself and I had crutches and a hovering mother helping me.

It isn't until he nears the top that I see the metal rod sticking out of the right side of his shorts where his leg should be. *Oh.*

I'm waiting for Miss to tear into him for being late. Instead, she gives him a smile as if she's a tween fangirl and he's her favorite pop star.

"Pierce!" She stands up to give him a bear hug. "I was afraid you'd changed your mind."

"I'm not sure how much help I can be," he says. "But I'm grateful to get more time on that equipment. Thank you."

"Everyone, this is Pierce," she tells the group. "He'll be assisting me." To him she adds, "How nice to have you and Rita both back together."

Pierce gives Rita a friendly grin, and I feel annoyed that I got such attitude for being late. It's not like I wanted a hug from Miss or anything, but come on. She and Rita are practically blushing at this guy.

Slumping down in my chair, I cross my arms. Sparky stands up and shakes Pierce's hand. "I saw the article in the paper and just want to say it's an honor." I look at Pierce more carefully but have no idea what Sparky's talking about.

"Sorry to disrupt." Pierce takes a chair from the corner and haltingly drags it to rest beside mine. He sits down more gracefully than I managed, gives me a quick wink, and whispers, "I just couldn't sit through that dang butterfly story again."

Without meaning to, I smile.

6

Unfortunately, Pierce's arrival only interrupts the sharing circle for a moment. Miss turns to the Asian girl with the eye patch and barks, "You're up, Polly."

Polly calmly tells us she's furious about getting her back messed up and losing her eye. In fact, her one-word description of herself is "pissed." I notice a thin pink scar dividing one of her perfect eyebrows and sneaking under her bangs, and in an odd way, I think it emphasizes her beauty.

"My boyfriend and I were camping together," she says in an even tone. "He'd crawled out of the tent and was off in the woods taking a leak when I woke up in the jaws of this giant black bear."

We give a loud collective gasp and Rita says, "Lord Jesus," and crosses herself briskly.

Polly continues with a grimace. "He ripped into our tent because my boyfriend had a tu—" She looks around at the group. "A . . . *lousy* bag of corn chips inside." She describes herself freaking out as the bear swung her in the air, sleeping bag and all. She'd screamed and punched and kicked, but the bear wouldn't let go. Finally, she went with her insane instinct to just go limp.

Apparently that was what did the trick. The bear figured she was dead and let her be, but not before he'd twisted her spine, rupturing two of her discs and cracking three ribs. Not to mention clawing her head and wrecking her eye. Without emotion, Polly tells us how staying still while she felt herself being eaten alive was the hardest thing she's ever had to do.

"My boyfriend got back too late to save me," she says. "And the worst part is, I'm pretty sure he's my soon-to-be-ex-boyfriend." She gestures to her patch with more emotion than she's shown the whole time. "One-eyed girls aren't too sexy."

That's the worst part? The guy dumping her? I make a mental note to not expect too much from Polly.

Rita reaches over and pats her hand. "Don't need more than half an eye to see that you're beautiful." She leans in and tells Polly, "If he's making you feel ugly, then give the guy a little Motörhead." Her voice goes deep and gravelly and she squints her whole face. "Tell him, *You can go to hell.*"

I see Pierce trying to stifle a laugh. "Is she for real?" I ask him under my breath.

"She loves '80s metal and calls herself a Jesus freak," he whispers. "But Rita's the most real person I know."

Miss slowly looks around, making eye contact with each of us. "In order to master your inner healing, you will—each one of you—need to face that thing that led you here. So, Polly, you'll obviously need to get back out there camping in the woods."

"You're joking, right?" Polly crosses her arms and juts out her delicate chin. "My boyfriend's the one who was into camping and he's never going again."

"It is a radical approach, I know, but nobody gets a Ulysses

Certificate of Healing without completing their recovery assignment," Miss says. "And I choose each challenge. Rita gets a pass since she successfully overcame cross-country skiing with the last group."

Looking around the circle, I try to figure out why any of us should care about some meaningless certificate of healing from this flaky woman.

Frank holds his palm up at Miss. "So, I'll be learning how to text while driving?"

A few of us laugh, but Miss seems to consider his question. "No, but you will need to get comfortable back in the driver's seat, Frank."

"I'm perfectly willing to go hiking again," says Sparky. "But I'd like to think I learned my lesson about doing it during a lightning storm."

"What do you think the odds are you'll be struck by lightning a second time?" Miss says. "All of you are statistically less likely to suffer another life-altering traumatic event."

"So you're saying it's only one accident per customer? You've clearly never met my brother." I can't wait for Mom to get me out of here. Leaning over, I whisper to Frank, "You've got two good legs. You should run."

He tries unsuccessfully to hold in a chuckle as Miss turns on me. "What's the matter, sweet cheeks?" she mocks. "You afraid your cheerleading skirt won't look good with a big ole scar on your leg?"

I spit out the word "cheerleading" as if it's a phlegm ball and rise out of my seat until Frankenfoot drags me back down.

Miss positions her body in my direction. "You can get mad at me if you want, but I'm not your greatest *struggle factor* right now. That bum leg of yours is."

"I can't believe you think I care about some stupid scar!" I'm furious. "You don't know anything about me. I used to hike and bike and climb all over these mountains." I gesture toward the Gunks. "These were *my* mountains. So, yeah, I'll always have a wicked scar running up my shin, but that's nothing compared to all the awesome stuff I can't do anymore."

Frustration stings my eyes. "What's the point of all this if I can't have my mountains? Now all I see is the long fall from every steep cliff." I lower my voice. "That's what crushes me. Not some stupid scar."

Pierce is watching me with a strange look on his face. I glare at him as if to say "And what the hell is *your* problem?" But he doesn't drop his gaze.

"And there you have it." Miss grins at me. "Your recovery challenge will need to help you overcome your fear of falling."

I stare at her. "I'm pretty sure my aversion to falling is permanent."

Miss just ignores me. "We must all commit to supporting each other in inner as well as outer healing. That means, Polly, we'll all join you on your recovery challenge in the woods." Polly gives a snort as I try to imagine this haphazard crew camping in the woods together.

Miss crosses her arms with finality. "It is the Ulysses way."

Polly says, "You do realize Ulysses is the dude who took ten freaking years to get home from the Trojan War, right?" I reconsider Polly's potential as we pack up our inner feelings and head inside for the outer healing part of our session. *At least this freak show is half over.*

We're led through the glass doors off the deck and I take in the giant open floor space. Equipment that looks like it could be from some elaborate gym in the future is lined up along the varnished walls, and soft trippy music streams around us. We're greeted by a skinny blond woman wearing pink workout wear and a matching glossy pink smile.

She gestures toward the massive space like a game show hostess and announces, "Welcome to the Ulysses Outer Healing Wellness Center."

The pink Barbie doll glides around demonstrating how all of the equipment works. I can't imagine what sort of hospital mixup led to her and Miss becoming sisters.

Pierce heads directly for a cluster of exercise bikes and mounts one. I watch him clip his sneakers into the pedals and start riding as if the bike can take him someplace he's in a rush to be.

Workout Barbie guides me to lie down on the mat and shows me a series of leg lifts and stretches that I'm supposed to do three times a day. "Envision healing. Envision strength. Envision power," she chants in my ear as I obligingly do cheater sit-ups and envision quitting.

When she leans over to help me change position, I notice a shirt tag peeking out from the back of her collar. It makes me almost like her for a moment until she introduces me to these hateful things called toe crunches. Breathing through clenched teeth, I focus on seeing Jay this afternoon.

Time runs so thick in this place I feel like I'm stuck in a

Jell-O mold. Looking around I think, *Suspended with all the other fruits.*

I practically knock Mom over with my hug when I spot her talking with Miss out on the deck. Miss is doing a very nice job of pretending to be professional.

"So, how was it?" Mom asks as we climb into the car.

"Oh, I'm not coming back," I say matter-of-factly.

"Um, I'm pretty sure you are. I've put twelve weeks down on the credit card, and even with insurance paying half this place is pricey, Dyna, believe me."

I groan. I can picture her and Dad arguing over the cost in our crowded kitchen. Dad's shop, the Tattoo Guru, is the most successful tattoo parlor in town, and Mom does nicely selling her sewn creations, but our normal budget does not include therapy sessions run by insane people. "I'm sure you can get a refund, Mom. This really isn't my thing."

"Well, obviously it hasn't been your thing, Dyna," Mom says, laughing. "It's not as if a person wakes up one morning and decides, hey, I've got nothing better to do. I think I'll give physical therapy a shot." The image of Rita with her gray braids flashes in my mind.

"It's not the physical therapy part that sucks." I rub at the soreness in my leg. "It's all that touchy-feely sharing-circle crap. Actually, it's not even touchy-feely. It's just . . . twisted."

"Twisted?" Mom keeps her attention glued to the road.

"The lady running the place is nuts. She called me a

cheerleader." Mom snickers and I go on. "She expects us to all go camping with the girl who got attacked by a bear."

"A girl got attacked by a bear?"

"Yes, and Miss won't be happy until we all get eaten in the forest."

"You used to love camping when you were younger. Maybe you should open yourself to their methods. The article said they get the absolute best results anywhere." She looks at me. "Don't you want to get back to normal?"

"Trust me. This place is *not* a gateway to normal."

I launch in about Workout Barbie's pink assault on my vision and Mom holds up her hand to stop me. "You want to avoid getting your ankle fused, don't you?"

"Of course, but . . ."

"This place is your best bet." Her lips are set and I see a flash of her old temper. "Subject closed. New topic."

We ride in silence for a time until I realize something. "Wait a minute. School starts back up in another month. They won't excuse me from classes for three hours a day. I'll never graduate."

"Actually." Mom glances at me. "I've looked into home-schooling for your senior year and I think it could be a reasonable solution."

I try to imagine never going back to New Paltz High School as Mom explains that nowadays everything's done online. "It will give you time to really focus on your healing."

I have to admit, a free pass from senior year does sound sort of awesome. No dealing with crowded hallways on my crutches. No dealing with crowded hallways period.

But then I'll be stuck at the Ulysses Center with all their inner-outer healing crap. I imagine myself sealed in glass, as helplessly trapped as Miss's doomed blue butterfly.

"Did you notice Miss Brauhn's pendant?" It's the type of thing Mom loves.

"God, yes," she says wistfully, as if that's what convinced her the center is legit. "It was a perfect Karner butterfly specimen."

"You mean Ulysses, right? It's a Ulysses butterfly."

"I think I know a Karner when I see one, Dyna. I've sketched enough of them." Mom laughs. "They're common around here, and you'd have to go to Australia to find a Ulysses. They look a lot alike, but that was definitely a Karner."

"Oh. Great."

Any hope that the Ulysses Center might not be a total waste of time flies right out the open car window.

7

When we pull up to the house Jay's black Subaru is parked in the driveway as far to the left as possible. He's in the driver's seat tapping at his electronic tablet, but once he sees us he tucks it under his arm and jogs over to open my door. He and Mom exchange friendly "hellos" as she heads into the house.

"How was it?" Jay helps/carries me out of the car.

"Ugh." I crinkle my nose. "Instead of Ulysses they should call it the Useless Center."

"Total waste, huh?"

"Well . . . I *did* meet this cute guy." I twirl my hair wickedly. Jay pantomimes using his tablet like a knife to stab himself in the heart and I laugh. "Only one cute guy for me."

He rewards me with a kiss and eases me onto the lounger on our low front deck. His tablet is still in his hand, and I teasingly reach over and jab the home button. The thing he was working on flashes open and I stop.

"What is that?"

Jay looks down and seems flustered as he clicks back to his home screen.

"No, I want to see." With a sigh he reopens the file and hands me his tablet.

I stare at the scene. The overgrown trees. The sparkling water. Those crazy arching rails. It's the swim hole. I press my lips together and rub at the spot where Frankenfoot swallows my leg. Whisper the word "There."

Jay flinches. "I'm so sorry." He tries to ease the tablet out of my hands, but I hold tight.

I read the caption he's written out loud. "'This place is alive. The trees look like we've just caught them playing a game of freeze tag.'"

I smile. "Journalist my ass. You're a poet."

"That was just a stupid thought I jotted down that day," he says. "I assure you, I am not damaged enough to be a poet."

"So, what were you doing with this?"

Jay takes the tablet from me and mumbles, "Just something I'm messing around with." Louder he says, "But I want to hear about your morning. How was tea and crumpets?"

With a British accent I say, "I discovered clotted cream is not at all as disgusting as it sounds. In fact, it's quite lovely on scones."

"Well then," Jay mocks. "You should try putting in a request for it at the New Paltz High cafeteria. Of course, their version will have actual clots."

"Bloody hell," I say. "I am *so* over high school." Jay laughs and I shake my head. "Oh, but I'm not kidding. Come September, I'm going to be homeschooled!" Saying it out loud for the first time makes it sound like really good news.

Jay looks crestfallen.

I ask, "What's wrong?"

"I kind of thought we'd, you know, be like a power couple working our way through senior year together."

"That's sweet. But honestly, I've never really fit in there."

"But now you fit with me." Jay's green eyes meet mine.

"True. But you're missing the point." I think a minute, trying to come up with a way to explain it. "I feel like . . . like I've been stuck watching some really boring movie for years and years and now I finally have permission to walk out early."

Jay laughs and kisses the top of my head. "Okay, I get it. School's not for everyone."

He plans on getting into Columbia's journalism program, and I feel ashamed for not having lofty Ivy League aspirations. My only solid goal was to hike the Appalachian Trail right after graduation and now that's clearly off the schedule.

Jay says, "Tell me more about this hippy-dippy place that's stealing you away from me."

I sigh. "The workout stuff is nothing I can't handle. But there's this stupid group therapy thing and everyone's so, I don't know . . . tragic?"

Jay leans forward to listen as I describe each person. His eyes widen as I tell him about Polly and her bear attack. Sparky captures his interest as well, but when I get to describing Pierce I pause a moment. I don't really know anything about him.

"This one guy is sort of assisting with the group," I say. "He's a bit older than us and has a prosthetic leg, but I have no clue what his story is."

Jay closes his eyes and lifts his face to the sun as if trying to remember something. I want to kiss his blond eyelashes. "Is the guy's name P-something? Perry?" He snaps his fingers and answers himself. "Pierce!"

"That's it. Pierce."

"There was a huge article in the *New Paltz Times* three or four months ago about some kid who lost a leg. I remember it because a letter I wrote to the editor about the Earth Day parade ran in the same issue."

"What happened to him?"

"Oh, sure, don't ask me about getting my letter published or anything," Jay says.

"Right, because the *New Paltz Times* is so selective about what it prints on its letters page." I shove him and he laughs.

"Apparently, Pierce is only nineteen and he's already some sort of war hero."

"What?" I'm shocked, because the blue-eyed guy with dark, shaggy hair who hobbled onto the deck this afternoon does not match the term "war hero" even a little bit. It does, however, explain Sparky jumping up to shake his hand.

"He graduated a year or two ago. He went to school in Highland, otherwise we would probably have known him." Jay shakes his head. "The article said he earned a Purple Heart for saving another soldier from burning to death when their Jeep caught fire. That's how he lost his leg. Just crazy."

"Wow," I say, and Jay starts snapping his fingers.

"If I got an interview with that guy I could write a killer piece about his experience! A fallen soldier's point of view. He can be my Christopher McCandless."

The book that Jay gave me relates the true story of McCandless's life. I'm only about halfway through it, but I already know he renamed himself Alexander Supertramp, gave away all his money, headed into the wilds of Alaska, and ended up dead. Jay credits the author, Jon Krakauer, with using *Into the Wild* to turn the guy into a modern-day hero. "McCandless idolized nature and didn't respect how dangerous it could be, and it killed him," Jay says now. "I can do something similar in an article about Pierce's ideals costing him his leg. He'll make the ultimate hero. Any chance you could get me an interview?"

"I don't really know him yet," I say.

"That's okay." He smiles. "Maybe you can ask in a couple of weeks. Just work on getting close to him for me."

I have to admit I'm a little curious what Pierce's story is. It probably would make an interesting article. I nod and tell Jay, "I'll see what I can do."

8

The next day is a bit overcast, but the seven of us are sitting out-side on the Ulysses deck in order to capitalize on the "better flow of energy," according to Miss. *Obviously*.

"Today we'll be revisiting our actual traumas in closer detail," she announces, and I cringe. I'm not like Harley, who loves to mono-logue about his near-deaths, showing scars and lumpy bones as narrative illustrations. I will never enjoy talking about my accident.

Smiling, Miss says, "Pierce, why don't you go first and show the group how it's done?"

He squints at his clasped hands and begins. "Being in Af-ghanistan is like living in a giant hourglass filled with sand. No air to breathe. Only heat, and shifting time. On the day of my accident it's hot as always and our Jeep is loaded down with gear. We're trying to blaze through this zone before sundown and Mickey's joking around as he drives, making up some goofy rap song about killing bad guys. All of a sudden he yells, 'Incom-ing!'" Pierce swallows. "I don't even see what direction the attack is coming from. The Jeep is just . . . rolling over and over. The windshield's gone dark with sand.

"We land hard and flames are everywhere. The next thing I know I'm swimming toward daylight with everything I've got. I'm disoriented and trying not to pass out from the heat, just . . . lost. And then I look down and see Mickey." Pierce's eyes flash wildly as his hands knead each other. Miss leans over to put a palm on his shoulder and he goes on. "I realize the Jeep's on its side and Mickey's slumped against the steering wheel."

I glance around the circle and see everyone's leaning forward. Like we're all hoping for a better ending than the one we know must be coming.

Pierce's breathing is heavy as he says, "So, I don't think. I cut the seat belt. Grab Mickey . . . around his chest." He curls his forearms up, pantomiming the rescue. His T-shirt is dark with sweat under his arms. "And I pull him toward the light." He pauses and then rushes his words together. "The two of us got out but I didn't get clear before the Jeep's gas tank blew everything sky-high." He pats his prosthetic. "Taking my leg along with it."

The woods that wall in the deck are thick with silence. The birds must be expecting rain. Holding their breath. I'm trying to picture the desert and

the heat and

the burning Jeep swallowing his leg.

I lay a hand on mine, grateful it's still attached.

"Okay, Pierce, that was good," Miss says. "You've certainly come a long way since that first session when you couldn't even talk about being overseas."

Pierce rubs the back of his neck.

She says, "Would you mind telling us exactly what was going through your mind when the Jeep blew up?"

He looks at her for a beat then cups his hand to the side of his mouth, tilts his head up and calls out, *"Ooooh shiiiiit!"*

Frank lets out a loud laugh, and I feel like clapping, but Miss just says, "Fine. We'll go around the circle now. Starting with Dyna." *I need to find a new seat.*

With a groan I close my eyes and reach back in my mind to that sweltering day. I dig up the bright image of the cliff flying past me, the blur of Jay, water coming too fast. "This is stupid." I open my eyes.

"This is important," Miss says in a soothing voice which, coming from her, sounds pretty sinister.

I close my eyes again and play along. "Okay, so it's a gorgeous summer day and I'm at the best swim hole on the planet. I've just done this beautiful freestyle rock climb to a cliff about sixty feet in the air." I take a breath at the memory. "Anyway, I decide to crawl back down using these weird metal tracks angled from the top of the cliff. I plan to jump into the swim hole once I climb low enough, but I'm still near the top. And the water below me is . . . too shallow." I clear my throat. "The wood plank I'm sitting on starts to pull loose from its stakes." I peek one eye open, see Rita nod her gray head encouragingly, and I snap it shut again, trying to concentrate.

In my mind

I'm sitting on a rotted chunk of fate.

It lets loose and

the rusty rails float up and out of my reach.

I'm overwhelmed by hopelessness.

Falling.

I open my eyes. "I must've passed out because I don't really remember anything after that."

Miss looks disappointed, but Pierce reaches over to pat my hand. *He knows I'm lying.* I don't know where that thought comes from, but suddenly I'm convinced Pierce can read minds. Can read my mind. I don't look at him.

Sparky is up next and starts to describe the sensation of having three hundred thousand volts course through his body. I stare at the empty bird feeders and focus on the way I feel when I'm tucked into the perfect crook of Jay's arm.

He drove me here today and is off somewhere writing on his tablet until I finish. Mom is in New York City buying material and Harley's skydiving out at the Ranch, so Jay and I plan to spend the afternoon making out and playing dirty-word Scrabble at my house.

When I corral my mental presence back into the healing circle, Polly has already shared and Frank is pantomiming being flung around the inside of his truck. He's wearing a T-shirt today that says STUBBY, and he flails his arms and legs comically as he turns his terrible accident into a hilarious story. I let myself join in laughing with the rest of the group.

Next Rita gives what she calls her "testimony," which consists of her describing her fall while skiing, but with extra details that make the whole experience sound like a huge blessing from Jesus. When she gets around to "Amen" we all go inside for physical therapy.

I do a few stretches and foot rolls on the mat before climbing on the exercycle and knocking the tension down to the lowest setting. Slowly, I churn Frankenfoot around as I pick at my thumbnail.

Frank is test-driving a prosthetic arm so Workout Barbie gives him extra attention while making her rounds. I picture her closet looking like the inside of a cotton-candy machine.

The cycle beside me whirs to life. I look over to see Pierce pedaling briskly with his good leg, a determined expression on his face. Like he's still searching for some war to win. Glancing at his screen, I see he's already climbing past 60 RPMs. I'm ashamed to note my machine's display is still blinking with the big red words "Begin Workout Now."

I awkwardly churn Frankenfoot a little faster until my exercycle finally registers that my workout has, in fact, begun. Beside me Pierce continues to pedal faster and punches his resistance up to six. Annoyed, I give my tension button two jabs and immediately feel burning in my good leg since it's the one doing most of the work. My speed drops again and the blinking machine mocks: "Begin Workout Now." With a grunt I push faster and finally get the taunting message to go away. Struggling to keep my pace above 33 RPMs, I notice Pierce is zipping along at over 80. Droplets of sweat start to form at his temples.

I push myself to 45 RPMs, which is still pretty slow, but a shot of pain prods my ankle. "Oh!" I wince, and Pierce breaks his concentration to look over.

"You okay?" he asks, which is sort of hilarious. I mean, there he is cycling with *one leg* and all I can think about is how much I want to stop pedaling and go home.

"Sure." I press on.

I glance over and see the slightest smile haunting the corner of Pierce's mouth. He catches me looking, raises an eyebrow, and begins to pedal even faster. I give an involuntary gasp as he punches his tension up to nine, but I'm too afraid of reinjuring my ankle to bump up my speed or tension any more.

But I don't slow down either.

By the time I open the door to Jay's Subaru I've regained my breath but feel weak from the neck down.

"Good workout today?"

I sink into the passenger seat with a groan. "They pushed me really hard." As I say the words I realize Workout Barbie actually didn't speak to me at all. She only smiled when she came by and noted my numbers on the exercycle.

Pierce is walking unevenly across the parking lot and our eyes meet through the windshield.

"Oh wow, is that him?" Jay reaches up and presses the control to open the sunroof.

Pierce moves right past my window, and our eyes stay locked until the last moment when he gives a long slow blink and then looks away. "Um, yeah. That's him." Turning my head, I watch him step onto a worn path leading into the woods.

Jay puts his arm around my seat and twists to back up the car. "No rush, but it will be so great if you can get that interview for me." I nod, wondering how far Pierce has to walk home each day.

"Want to go for a stroll later?" I ask as Jay pulls away from Ulysses. The sun has finally made an appearance through the clouds.

"Sure, Dyna-girl." He smiles. "But first there's an orange couch that has our names on it. I'm going to make sure you rest and recover before releasing you back into the wild."

An hour later we're in my living room with a reality show droning on in the background as we play dirty-word Scrabble. The game awards triple points for any words related to sex, and I'm winning. Jay claims I have an advantage because I have a raunchier vocabulary than he does. "Not that I'm complaining," he clarifies as he leans in for a kiss. He hasn't mentioned us going for a walk, but my ankle still twinges a bit from my workout.

Besides, once I pull off turning the word "late" into "titillate," Jay can't keep his hands off me. He gently props Frankenfoot on a pillow safely out of the way and the two of us sink into our delicious make-out position that makes time get all floaty.

We're lost in each other until Harley bursts in calling, "Heads up!"

Jay is slingshot to the other end of the couch and pretends to be absorbed in watching the commercial playing on television. I can't help but laugh as I wipe my mouth and ask Jay, "How did you get over there so fast?"

Leaning over our abandoned Scrabble game, Harley takes the letter *R* from my rack and adds it to the word "bone." "Hey, look"—he grins at Jay— "'boner.' Triple word score." Jay blushes and my brother gives a low whistle as he heads up the stairs.

"I didn't realize how late it was," Jay says as he briskly scoops the Scrabble tiles into their pouch. "I'd better get going."

"What's wrong? Nervous my dad will walk in and think you're corrupting me?"

"Who's corrupting whom here, Miss Titillate?" He grins and kisses me while his hand caresses my arm. We linger a moment, but pull apart before things start up again. "I need to work out before dinner," he says. "And by the way, my family is seriously torturing me about meeting you."

"I know, I know." I gesture to Frankenfoot. "When I'm ready."

My legs are stiff when Jay helps me up from the couch. We share a swoony kiss at the door and I promise to meet his family soon-*ish*. Besides perfect-sounding parents, I imagine Jay's three protective older sisters "weeding out the weak" with some method that's as emotionally crippling as my father's.

It turns out Jay didn't need to rush out, since Dad is working late at the Tattoo Guru anyway. When Mom gets home from the city, we decide to make sandwiches for dinner. It's a sound move, considering the deficiency of our combined cooking skills.

"I ordered your homeschool supplies before I left this morning," Mom tells me as she piles tomatoes and kale on the cutting board. "They should be here in two weeks."

"Great." I start spreading tuna on slices of whole wheat. "I can get a nice early jump on the workload."

The two of us spent a lot of time on the computer searching for the perfect self-paced homeschool program. Now she just needs to go down to the high school and sign me out. To be honest, we were both a little surprised at how easy it has been to make the switch.

"I thought only pregnant girls dropped out of school." Harley reaches over my shoulder to grab two sandwich halves off the counter. He gives me a glazed-over grin and bites into half of one.

"I am not dropping out of school." I glance at Mom's back end sticking out of the fridge and hiss at him, "She's going to see you're baked."

He whispers, "Dad's the bulldog around here," and laughs as he shoves the rest of the sandwich half in his mouth.

"Don't forget we go to the doctor's after Ulysses next Friday," Mom calls from the fridge. "Aren't you excited they might be changing your cast?"

"That's a week and a half away, Mom. I think I'll pace myself on getting excited."

Harley says, "You must be jonesing for a good climb by now."

I shoot pickaxes at him with my eyes, but he just gestures to the sandwich I'm cutting. "You planning to eat that?"

With a sigh I announce I'm going to eat in front of the TV.

"Don't forget to take your vitamins." Mom shakes a baggie filled with large brown and tan capsules. Harley walks haltingly from the kitchen with a bemused expression on his face, but Mom's concern stays focused solely on me.

An hour later I climb into bed and pick up *Into the Wild*. I'm completely rooting for Alexander Supertramp at this point, despite the fact that I know he's going to die.

Reading through heavy lids I come across a postcard Krakauer has quoted that Alex sent to friends in North Dakota. It says: *Hey Guys! This is the last communication you shall receive from me. I now walk out to live amongst the wild. Take care, it was great knowing you. Alexander.*

I picture Alex filled with giddy anticipation as he forged his own way in the world. Living his life completely on his terms. Diving headfirst into the wilderness.

Closing the book, I slide my thumb along my inner wrist. I've always imagined words tattooed there. *Not all who wander are lost.* They fade in my mind as I toss the book on my nightstand and turn off the lamp.

When I shut my eyes I see myself

hurtling toward the water again.

Too fast.

Flipping the light back on, I bury my head halfway under my pillow and try to block out the scene Miss seems obsessed with having me remember. No matter what she thinks, it must be possible to have a perfectly normal life after a trauma without sharing every nuance of feeling with a roomful of strangers.

I shove my thoughts under the bed, but it takes me over an hour to fall into a dreamless sleep.

9

"What's the deal with Whitebread sneaking around here when I'm not home?" Dad greets me when I come down for breakfast. Mom and Harley both love sleeping in, so mornings are sort of our thing.

"Good morning to you, too," I say mock-sweetly while clutching the kitchen counter. I grimace at the soreness in my legs as I hop toward the fridge.

"Sorry, Dyna." Dad feigns chipperness. "Good morning, sweetheart!" His voice drops back to his usual baritone. "Now, what's with Whitebread—"

"Fine. Fine," I cut him off as I slide the milk onto the table. "Jay's not sneaking around. And maybe he wouldn't avoid you if you didn't work so hard at intimidating him."

"My job." Dad shrugs.

"There's nothing wrong with me hanging out here with my *boyfriend*." I emphasize the word just to watch Dad's eye twitch. "It's not like I can do any of my usual summertime activities." I stretch to grasp a box of cereal in the pantry.

"You want me to make you some eggs?" Dad offers.

I shake my head. "No thanks." Dad cooks amazing omelets, but I'm really hungry and if I let him get started, I may starve to death waiting for one of his culinary masterpieces.

"So, let's talk about this do-it-yourself education of yours," he says, as I pour cereal into my bowl on the counter. "Are you sure you can handle all that work on your own?"

"Homeschooling's going to be a piece of cake." Dad's nostrils flare out and I immediately realize this was the wrong thing to say.

"That's what you want your education to be? A 'piece of cake'?"

"No, it's not like that." I try to backtrack. "Dad, there's all sorts of research showing how homeschooled kids are high achievers. Besides . . ." I clutch the bowl to my chest and walk my hand along the counter toward the table. "You saw how great Harley did in high school and what's he doing with his life now?" It's true. Harley's so smart he got excellent grades without even trying, but he's been killing off brain cells since graduation.

Dad sighs and studies his oatmeal, and I'm hit with guilt. Harley not living up to his potential is a sore spot, especially since he was offered several academic college scholarships. Instead he enrolled in the nearby Culinary Institute of America, claiming he wanted to be a chef at the Mohonk Mountain House. It seemed like a cool plan, but then, half a semester later, he discovered skydiving and quit. The supermarket is just the latest in a string of local McJobs he's had over the past two years. He's developed a reputation for not showing up for work on clear sunny days.

"I'm not talking about your brother," Dad says. "Dyna, if

you're looking at homeschooling as an easy way out, well then, that's not the girl I've raised."

I blink at the sting. "Homeschooling was Mom's idea."

"Okay, firstly, I love the woman to death, but your mother has completely lost her cheese over your accident. I'm only going along with this crazy voodoo therapy place to keep the peace."

I say with fake ditziness, "I can't understand why talking about my feelings isn't making my ankle better yet."

Dad lets out a chuckle that fills me.

"I have to go camping with them next Saturday," I groan. "What is that about?"

He raises a fuzzy eyebrow at me. "Since when do you not like the outdoors, Dyna Glider?"

"It's not that. Some girl in my group got mauled by a bear and now we're all supposed to go hold her hand out in the woods. Like that's going to prove something."

"Okay, so the asylum is being run by the lunatics. I get that. But going camping won't kill you. And neither would high school. Maybe you can stick with therapy until school starts and then we can find you some sort of evening and weekend sessions."

I knew homeschooling was too easy.

I think fast. "Dad, I'm supposed to graduate this year, and with hiking and climbing out of the picture I don't even know what's next. Homeschooling will give me a chance to figure out what to do with my life. I'll work hard on my education as I explore other interests."

Dad grumbles, "If you think for one moment that watching television on the couch next to that moldy slice of white bread counts as *exploring other interests*, then you need to think again."

"Please stop," I plead. "If Jay knew you called him Whitebread he'd probably break up with me."

"Good." Dad looks pleased and I slap his arm right below the naked angel tattoo. I always ignore the fact that the angel has Mom's face on it. "I'll stop calling him Whitebread when he faces me and starts acting a little whole grain or rye." Dad chuckles. "Maybe shows a nice swirl of pumpernickel?"

"Oh yeah?" I say, flustered. "Well, I think Jay is *Wonder*bread." Dad laughs so hard at that I eventually crack up, too. "Okay, so that didn't sound so dorky in my head," I say. "But Jay's really a nice guy."

Dad grunts and mimics me in a girly voice, "Nice guy." He levels me a look. "You are much too special for some *nice guy*, Dyna."

"He's a *special* guy, too, Dad."

"The only thing that kid has going for him is the fact that he's ass over tits for you, sweetheart. But you need to ask yourself this . . . What do *you* see in *him*?"

I crinkle my nose. "I like him."

"Well, a person who's in love with you can be a pretty likable thing." Dad leans over his bowl and adds, "Especially when you're feeling vulnerable." He points his spoon at me as if he's just made a startling point and shovels a heaping bite of oatmeal into his mouth.

I swallow my smart-ass response with a spoonful of cereal and the thought *He's just upset to see his little Dyna Glider so in love*.

10

Polly clutches a can of "bear spray" that's almost as big as her head as she climbs from the van at the campsite. It's only four o'clock and we're all prisoners of the outdoors until tomorrow morning.

I'm thinking this excursion is too soon. Polly hasn't exactly had any sort of healing circle *breakthrough* in the past two weeks of sessions. In fact, she usually spends her sharing time talking about getting dumped by her ex-boyfriend.

She's huddled beside the Ulysses van now, hugging her backpack with her bear spray cocked and ready. Her beautiful features are drawn in worry as her one eye darts back and forth.

The whole gang's here, except for Workout Barbie, who doesn't do recovery assignments. Too bad we'll miss out on her Camp Barbie accessory kit. I picture a pink sleeping bag, pink lantern, and pink binoculars lined up neatly beside a shiny pink plastic tent.

Miss offered to let Rita take a pass, but Rita seems thrilled to be here, with her braids poking out from her faded black Mötley Crüe baseball cap. Meanwhile, Miss refused to let me stay home despite the fact that I'm still adjusting to the new ankle brace I got at the doctor's yesterday. It's basically a dorky white plastic form that attaches with Velcro straps, and we're calling it Son of Frankenfoot. It doesn't come up as high on my calf, so now the top inch of raw scar shows when I wear shorts, which is most of the time.

The doctor said I'm healing well and told me I'm cleared to put 50 percent pressure on my foot with the new brace, but I miss the sturdiness of Frankenfoot. Mom got me a funky birchwood cane that's actually sort of cool-looking as far as geriatric accessories go, but I brought my crutches camping. The doc said, "Let pain be your guide," and my pain is guiding me to stay the hell off my foot.

I'm sitting at the picnic table with my backpack on my lap waiting for Miss to finish putting up the girls' tent. Pierce walks by with an armload of tent poles and nods my way. "Hey, Dyna, you mind gathering some kindling?"

I'm not sure if I'm more annoyed by the fact that he's asked me to do something when I don't even want to be here, or if I'm just pissed because he's trying to give me the girly job of collecting twigs.

"Let Polly pick up sticks." I toss my bag onto the ground. Grabbing one of my crutches, I hobble over to give Miss a hand with the tent. Just because I haven't been camping in a while doesn't mean I don't know how to be useful.

Banging a tent peg into the hard ground with a hammer, I look back just as Pierce finishes putting up the boys' tent with a flourish. I ask Miss, "Hey, do you need me to chop wood or something after this?"

"Glad to see you're embracing the struggle, Dyna," she says.

"Of course we need plenty of firewood, and the workout will do you good."

Which is how I end up trying to keep my weight off my bad leg as I hack away at logs with the giant ax Miss gave me. Nothing is cooperating. I feel Pierce watching me but refuse to make eye contact. Finally, he comes over and offers to teach me how to chop firewood.

I try to brush off his help, but falter as I swing down. The ax slips away from the wood and Pierce bends and catches it near the head after it barely misses Son of Frankenfoot. I'm shocked by his strength and speechless as he eases the ax from my hands.

"Whoa," he says. "May want to keep that leg, you'll get it working eventually."

I don't look at him, but I can feel his smile aimed at my neck. I try to act as if I nearly chopped my leg off on purpose. "I'm used to a hatchet," I explain.

"Oh, well, in that case, I think I brought one."

"That's okay. I'm getting the hang of it," I lie. I'm actually getting worse as my arms get tired, but I refuse to admit defeat to him. I grip the ax with new determination and will myself to channel a lumberjack.

Instead of laughing at me as I expect, he says, "Fine," and moves to stand close behind me. He puts one hand on my hip and covers my hands on the ax with the other. "What you want to do is find the seam in the wood and really lodge the ax in there hard." His voice flows through the curtain of my hair. "Then use the weight of it to do the work for you."

With a firm *thunk* he demonstrates this one-handed, while

my fists remain on the handle as decoration. The ax head buries itself in the wood. Pierce guides my hand in raising the ax and the log travels up with it. Together, we drive the ax down against the hard ground, and sure enough, the blade buries deeper into the log. The split is nice and wide now, and it's with satisfaction that I lift the ax to deliver the death blow.

I feel Pierce ease off my hip as he allows me the victory.

Crack! The log separates and I grin. "See that?" I call out.

"Good job," Miss says, as she throws a handful of kindling into the fire pit. Somehow, that chore doesn't seem so girly anymore.

"I think you've got this." Pierce gives a hop backward before turning to help with the giant red cooler Frank and Sparky are carrying. Frank's fake arm sticks out from under the lid so it looks like there's a body crammed inside. I can't help but laugh.

Miss recites a little motivational speech about how proud she is we're all supporting Polly, and then she asks Sparky if he minds getting the fire going.

Despite our sadistic therapist's taste for irony in having the burn-scarred guy build the fire, I'm glad Sparky starts on it right away. We're a week and a half into August, but it's a little chilly up here in the woods by the time he gets it rolling.

The smell of the campfire sets off something deep and happy in my brain. Like a photo album just fell open, I'm remembering a dozen camping trips with my family all at once. I smile at the image of me and Harley catching frogs as Mom and Dad argue about where to set up the tent. The warm days of swimming in lakes and cool nights roasting marshmallows blend together in my mind.

After we've slogged through the rituals of cooking, eating, and cleaning up, the group sits on canvas camp chairs holding our hands toward the licking flames. Polly is busy scanning the black tree line, even though it's too dark to see anything by now.

I'm wedged between Miss and Polly and my leg refuses to find a comfortable position in the chair I'm in. As I shift my weight my crutches slide down with a loud clatter.

Before any of us know what's happening, Polly jumps up, spins around, and frantically starts spraying her bear spray into the empty air behind her chair.

Pssssssssht echoes through the woods as a growing cloud of fog shoots out of the nozzle.

Polly grunts as she continues gripping the can with both hands, elbows locked. The mist spreads and my nose starts to sting with a spicy stench that reminds me of wasp spray. I watch through burning eyes as a blurry Miss just sits there observing calmly. The rest of us seem stuck to our chairs.

Everyone, that is, except Pierce. He bounds over to Polly and grabs her hands from behind. Polly's face contorts with fear and she tries to turn her spray in his direction. I hold my breath, waiting for him to get a faceful of bear spray, but Pierce continues to hold her hands firmly, all of his muscles flexed.

He whispers something in her ear.

Finally, the spray stops, her arms go limp, and he eases the can out of her shaking hands. Sounds of coughing and gagging fill the air and everyone rubs at their eyes.

Polly stands frozen in the center of the circle while tears from her good eye glint in the firelight. Her face crumples and she turns to bury it in Pierce's shoulder. He keeps an arm around her, smoothing her hair with his palm as he stares into the trees. It's as if he's watching an intense scene play out in the blackness that only he can see.

My throat feels like it's closing up and my sweet campfire memories wither and curl from the sharp smell. If Polly had actually sprayed someone directly I'm pretty sure we'd be on our way to the hospital about now.

"Well, then." Miss looks around the circle. "That was some breakthrough, huh? Good job, Polly." Her face pops into a wide smile.

Polly raises her head from Pierce's shoulder and shoots her a one-eyed glare of death.

"And, Pierce?" Miss pulls him back to the present. "I told you those reflexes of yours weren't a curse." He gives a short laugh and shakes his head.

The coughing slowly morphs into an uncomfortable silence laced with loud frog-chirping, and Pierce and Polly untangle and sit back down. He pokes at the fire with a long stick as she glances in his direction from time to time.

Rita is first to head to bed, commenting that she's had a lovely time but she's exhausted. Miss excuses herself soon afterward. When Sparky announces he's going fishing in the morning, Frank asks to tag along. They discuss inhuman wake-up hours as they drag themselves from their chairs. Based on their groaning and stretching, I'm pretty sure the fish will be safe come dawn.

Frank takes his prosthetic arm in his opposite hand and gives a salute good night before making his way toward the guys' tent. Sparky stops and turns to Polly, his smooth face shining in the firelight: "Polly, I think you are being incredibly courageous."

She glares at him a moment but his earnest expression must move her. Instead of giving a snarky comment, she nods at him before getting up and walking over to the cooler. I see a flicker in Sparky's eyes as he says good night. *He likes her.*

When Polly asks Pierce if he wants something to drink he calls, "No thanks," and moves to the chair next to mine. Glancing over at Polly, he puts a hand on my arm and whispers, "Stay up with me?"

I keep my expression neutral as I stare into the fire.

"Polly's in shock." His voice is so low I strain for every word. "She's vulnerable right now, but I'm not ready to go to bed yet. I don't think she and I should be alone together."

Is he telling me that he doesn't trust himself alone with Polly? Or is he saying he's afraid she may come on to him? I glance over at her as she settles back into her chair. She looks gorgeous in the firelight. He probably can't resist her but doesn't want to take advantage. He picked me for backup.

I nod at him as if it's no big deal, and so now it's just the three of us sitting around the fire. Based on the looks Polly's giving, she seems determined to outlast me and have Pierce to herself.

I smile at her sweetly. "Stars look great tonight, huh?"

My recent and vast experience with insomnia has equipped

me for this very moment. I may not have Pierce figured out, but I know that tonight I won't be letting him down.

I blink awake to the sound of birds celebrating daylight.

When I try to move I realize I must've dozed off in the chair by the fire. Someone's placed my sleeping bag over me and it slips down and catches on the armrest. I note with satisfaction that Polly must've given up and gone to bed at some point during the night. All the other chairs are empty except for the one next to me where Pierce sits sleeping.

The two of us talked late into the night while Polly brooded, poking at her cell phone and complaining about having no service. I ended up telling Pierce more about my accident than I'd intended. More than I thought I'd ever tell anyone.

Pierce could completely relate to my adrenaline-fueled experience, and it actually felt good to share it. He confirmed my sense of losing a part of myself, although, he jokingly pointed out, he did *literally* lose a part of himself. Tapping his prosthesis with a flashlight, he made it *clink* and said, "This does not define who I am." He looked at me and shrugged. "Still figuring that out, mind you."

We bonded over how much it sucks when we have to pee in the middle of the night and can't run to the bathroom, and he told me that the reason he went with the metal-rod prosthetic was because he would've had to start shaving his good leg to match a leg-looking one. He held an invisible razor up to his shin with delicate fingers and batted his eyelashes at me. "Not happening."

I asked him what his recovery assignment was and he told me Miss had them all go to a massive paintball field out in Platte-kill.

"We had this crazy-intense battle to help me get over the fear that I was going to get triggered and freak out from PTSD."

"I can't really picture Rita wearing camouflage and running around with a paintball rifle."

"She was the only one who managed to shoot me." We both laughed.

"Did the challenge work?" I asked.

"Things got pretty heated, but I guess it was encouraging that I didn't lapse into a violent flashback of being in Afghanistan." He shrugged. "Miss is seriously into exposure therapy."

I leaned back to watch the stars through the tree branches. "Well, camping's not so bad."

Pierce and I melted into comfortable silence while the campfire slowly burned out. The outdoors worked its magic on me until I eventually fell asleep. But that's the amazing part. Sitting in the middle of the woods underneath the trees, I slept soundly in an uncomfortable camp chair. Something I haven't managed to do for weeks in my own bed at home.

Now I watch the rosy sunlight dance through the leaves and across Pierce's face until he starts to rouse. Wrinkling his nose and rubbing it with the back of his hand, he blinks a few times before turning his sleepy eyes on me.

In the morning light, I feel like I'm seeing the real him. The him that goes deeper than that guy who went overseas and rode through hell and got his leg blown off. His hair sticks up in tufts on one side and his jaw is darkened with slight stubble. For a moment, looking at each other, we're not cripples

or patients

or victims.

We are just a boy and a girl.

He blinks at me and my temperature hikes by a few degrees. I ignore the stiffness in my hip as I shift forward. The gaze of his light eyes remains steady. The cold morning air grows wide in my lungs.

I want him.

That thought is interrupted by the sound of a zipper unzipping. Miss comes whistling out of the girls' tent and the spell is broken.

I shake off my wild impulse.

Return to the awareness that I have a great boyfriend who I'll be seeing in a few short hours. Pierce draws down a mask of indifference and raises an eyebrow at me before scrambling up to help Miss get food out of the van.

One should never underestimate the power of the scent of bacon. It rouses the rest of the group quickly and everyone pitches in to finish cooking breakfast. Afterward, Frank and Rita have an impromptu bacon-eating contest while Sparky and Miss discuss the benefits of free-range eggs. Polly laughs and flips her hair at Pierce as he uses olive oil to clean the iron skillet.

When he's done he walks over to where I'm sitting, and Polly tosses me razored looks. I'm grateful Miss took away her can of bear spray.

"Thanks for staying up last night." More than hearing Pierce's whisper, I feel it. "I must've nodded off right after you did."

"No prob." I shrug. "Who covered me with my sleeping bag?"

He grins. "You're welcome."

So now all I can imagine is him placing the sleeping bag over me and maybe even watching me sleep a moment. *God, I hope I wasn't drooling.* I blush and look up at the sky, sort of an automatic response after watching the stars for so long last night.

"Time to break camp!" Miss announces. "Successful mission." She clamps one arm across Polly's shoulder. Judging by the way Polly continues glaring at Pierce and me, she doesn't agree with the mission's success. At all.

II

When Jay comes to pick me up for an early dinner, I'm feeling a little nervous, and it has nothing to do with sharing an inappropriate gaze with another boy. Today is his oldest sister's birthday, and his whole family is meeting at a sports restaurant in town called P&Gs. Jay practically begged me to come and I've run out of excuses.

When we get to the restaurant, the smiling blond clan is already packed into the biggest wraparound booth in the place. Their hearty greetings engulf me. Jay's mom slides deeper into the booth and pats the seat next to her. "Dyna's here," she says. "It's easier to get up and down on the end." I lean my crutches against the back of the bench and she rubs my arm briskly when I sit down.

Thankfully, Jay gets one of his sisters to change seats so he's in the chair on the end next to me. A football game plays on the flatscreen televisions throughout the restaurant and Jay explains that it's the first scrimmage game for their favorite college team.

"The Panthers are looking good this year," his mother announces, and the whole family cheers in unison as the blue and gold team makes a play. They're so enthusiastic, I find myself rooting as loud as the rest of them by the time our waitress shows up.

"Hey there, Dyna," she says.

Jay's mother eyes the tan girl with chewed-up nails and her long dreadlocks pulled into a fat bun. I try to place her.

Got it. She's friends with a few of my climbing buddies, and the two of us went on belay together once. "Hey, Jen. How's it going?" I say.

"I heard about your fall. Huge bummer."

"I'm hanging in there." I reach back to pat my crutches, and Jay interrupts us to order artichoke dip with pita for an appetizer.

In between eating heartily and cheering for the game, Jay's sisters tell me stories of his talent for finding stray animals needing care.

"Cats, baby chipmunks, turtles . . . you name it," his one sister says. "Every type of frail creature you could imagine came home with Jay."

He laughs. "And now I've moved up to a gorgeous girl who practically fell into my arms." His sisters clap and one of them says, "Awww," as Jay lifts my hand he's holding and kisses my palm.

"Anything *else* for dessert?" Jen says with amusement, and Jay's mother asks if she minds taking a picture of the whole table. We order cake and all sing Happy Birthday to Jay's sister and then go crazy when the Pittsburgh Panthers win the game.

Clearing our table, Jen tells me, "Hey, maybe I'll see you back climbing sometime. I remember you being a total badass on the mountain."

"It's not really my scene anymore." I joke drily, "Belay *off*."

Jay's dad was fairly quiet during dinner, but as we all say goodbye he tells me, "I have to admit I was a little skeptical. Jay has gone on about how *wild* you are, mountain biking and taking risks." At my cringe he laughs. "I'm glad to see my son was exaggerating. You two make a nice fit."

"Yes." I smile up at Jay's handsome face. "I believe we do."

When we get to my house, Jay walks me to the front door and moves in for a deep kiss. He gives a low *"Mmmm"* when I slide my body deliberately upward and press against him.

Whap! Whap! Whap! We're startled by a banging on the window near our heads. Harley grins maniacally through the glass and waggles his eyebrow ring up and down. I toss my big brother the bird as Jay opens the door and follows me inside. Dad sits in the living room leafing through some tattoo trade magazine while watching a cooking show.

"Hi, kids," he says gruffly. "Mom's upstairs. It's going to be an *Easy Rider* night." He glances up. "That's a movie, Jay. You're welcome to join us."

Jay stares at Dad as if there's a rifle aimed at his crotch.

"He'd love to stay," I say, squeezing Jay's hand.

"Right," Jay says. "Family movie night. Sounds great."

As I pull him into the kitchen I hear Dad mock, *"Family movie night."* Jay either doesn't hear him or else pretends he doesn't.

"Don't be nervous." I start pouring drinks. "My dad is just a big teddy bear underneath all the growling."

"Ha," Jay says. "More like an enormous grizzly bear protecting his precious cub."

Harley sidles up to Jay at the kitchen counter and quietly asks, "Care to watch stoned? It makes this movie way better."

"Seriously, Harls," I hiss. "Dad will bury your body in the backyard if he catches you getting high."

Jay says quickly, "No thanks, Harley."

"Suit yourself." My brother heads off to his bedroom to smoke a joint out the window.

Jay tells me he's running back to his car for his tablet. "I'll look up some *Easy Rider* trivia," he says. "Your dad will love that stuff."

Easy Rider is not just my parents' favorite film, it's a viewing ritual performed every summer and it's always followed up by a road trip. Harley and I used to try to figure out if Dad decides it's time for our trip and then has us watch *Easy Rider* to get everyone in the mood, or if he just can't help himself and has to head for the open road after watching it.

Twenty minutes later we're all settled in the living room and the older, curvy version of Columbia Studios' Lady Liberty is posing onscreen. Jay is telling Mom, "So, I guess *Easy Rider* introduced Jack Nicholson to the world."

She smiles. "Yes, this was Nicholson's first film."

"And apparently they didn't have a full script when they started," he says. "They made things up as they went along."

"That's right," says Dad. "Hired folks they found along the way, too."

Jay smiles at me and takes my hand in his. The beautiful

countryside scrolls by on our TV while Peter Fonda and Dennis Hopper embark on their motorcycle ride across America.

"You know, the apehangers look cool," Dad says to Jay. "But Fonda's fingers would've gone numb after a few hours riding with those sissy bars." I'm filled with warm feelings toward Dad for finally reaching out to my boyfriend.

Jay says, "I read on IMDb that Jack Nicholson actually broke one of Peter Fonda's ribs trying to stay on the back of that bike."

Dad squints over at Jay. "What the hell's an IMD-what?"

"It's a website, Dad," I say. "It gives all sorts of cool trivia about movies."

Dad grunts. "Everybody's an instant expert on everything."

Harley tries unsuccessfully to rein in his laughter and Jay gives a quick smile, but he doesn't relax as the movie itself veers into strangeness. Maybe it's Jay's presence, or perhaps it's the fact that there are a lot of boobs showing near the end, but as I sit watching I realize for the first time that *Easy Rider* is a stupid excuse for a road trip. And a ridiculously inappropriate family movie.

When the film ends, Jay gives Dad an awkward handshake that Mom rescues with a swooping goodbye hug. We walk out to his car and Jay gathers me in his arms in the dark and leans back against his driver's side door.

"Well, family day has been *done*," he says.

"Yes it has," I agree.

As we embrace I can feel him more than see him, which is

pretty sexy. I raise my face and extend my neck for my dose of spearmint. After a delicious moment of kissing, Jay pulls back and whispers, "It was a great day because I was with you."

"Me too," I say sleepily.

"Go tuck yourself into bed."

"Why don't you come tuck me in?"

"I'd love that." He looks toward the house. "But I'm thinking if I try it, the movie won't be the only thing that ends in a fiery explosion tonight."

I laugh and Jay kisses me again and helps me get situated on my crutches before sliding into his car. I wave a blind goodbye to his headlights as he drives away.

It's not until I'm climbing into bed that I realize I forgot to tell him about getting to know Pierce a little better. I pull my comforter up and decide that smoldering look he and I shared by the burned-out campfire will be less damning once I let Jay know the two of us talked.

I wonder what the deal is with that guy anyway. What could've made him enlist so young? No matter how cool he may have seemed last night, I'll bet Pierce is still really messed up.

I imagine him ever-so-casually covering me as I slept. That image cuts to a close-up of sleep drool running down my chin and I cringe.

Spending overtime with my therapy group clearly has me setting my compass due *crazy*.

12

It's so hot that Monday morning we should all be worshipping the trees around the deck for their shade. I glance over to where Pierce is studying his hands while Miss talks about what an awesome event occurred Saturday night when Polly doused our campsite with bear spray.

Polly says she's probably not going camping again anytime soon, but she admits her fear of the woods was a little out of control.

"I do feel more powerful after facing it," she says, and we all applaud.

"Woot!" Rita holds up Polly's arm in victory and proclaims, "Bad to the bone bitches!"

To keep with the theme of Polly's so-called breakthrough, Miss would like each of us to share about fear and the way it affects our lives.

"Dyna." I actually flinch at the sound of Miss saying my name. "Would you like to discuss your experience with fear?" I look around at the faces watching me and claw my mind for a response that will satisfy Miss without exposing a whole new personal issue for her to dissect.

"I guess I just have the same basic fears as everyone else," I say. "Fear of public speaking, fear of dying, fear of falling—"

"Ah, yes, your fear of falling," Miss interrupts. "We'll need to dig deep into that one since you're still repressing the memory of your accident."

Polly butts in, saying, "I thought I heard you talking about it by the campfire . . ."

"It's still really fuzzy," I say.

Miss leans toward me, and Pierce blurts, "Fear is a choice."

Miss is drawn to the light of Pierce's words like a moth and asks him to go on. I flash him a look of gratitude.

"We can't always block fearful thoughts," he says. "But we can choose how much we allow them to control our lives."

He continues talking about the power of fear, and I press back a cocktail of emotions as I'm forced to recognize the underlying anxiety I've felt since my fall. I've been doing my best to ignore it, but my mind pulses with quiet constant fear that contradicts everything I thought I knew about myself.

I'm glad when it's finally time for us to shift our focus to outer healing. Using my cane I shuffle inside with the others, where we discover we'll be working in pairs this week. Since Sparky and Frank have become lifelong buddies by now and Rita and Polly are the recently formed duo of Badass Bitches, I get paired with Pierce.

"Gimps with the gimps," he jokes, and I have to bite my lip to avoid smiling. Workout Barbie brings the two of us to the mats by the windows and shows us a series of stretches we're to do together.

When she's finished demonstrating, Pierce gestures for me to go first. I lie on my back with my good leg raised and he pushes firmly on the back of my thigh, pressing it toward my chest for the count of twenty. The stretch starts to burn but I don't react as I focus on the woods outside the window.

Switching to my injured leg, Pierce says, "Let me know if I go too far." I glance at him.

Mistake.

Miss has explained a phenomenon called pain paths, where once the brain has felt a particular pain it's easier for that pain to be perceived again. Kind of like a weird organic nerve memory that we need to overcome. I suddenly realize Miss is not completely full of shit, because the current that connected me to Pierce at the campsite is back. *Those eyes*. My insides liquefy as we look at each other.

He has a hold on every inch of me and I can't break the current until the count of twenty is finished and he releases my leg.

"Did you feel that one?" he asks, and I wonder for a split moment if he's talking about the look we just shared. Of course he's asking about my leg. I nod, trying to picture Jay holding my hand in that ambulance as Pierce and I continue stretching together.

When we're ready to switch places, he unstraps his prosthetic leg and removes it. Pulling off the rubber sock underneath, he slides everything to the side of the mat. Watching him feels oddly intimate. Grimly he lies back, holds his good leg up, and I move into position.

As I press against the back of his leg he watches the ceiling, face tough, and commands, "Harder!"

I dig into the mat and lunge my full weight against him. He

grunts in response and I back off, but his strong arms draw around me and pull me toward him. He holds me against himself, his leg sandwiched between us.

He's watching my lips and his breath is hot on my face. I feel a tremor run through him, but I don't know if it's from the strain of the stretch or if he's showing as much restraint as I am.

He wants me.

Everything is reduced

to our matched breathing,

until someone drops a barbell with a thud and

the rest of the room comes back into focus. Rita is talking intently to Polly beside a rack of weighted pulleys, and Frank is holding his prosthetic arm up for a fake high five from Sparky.

Pierce releases me from our embrace. I clear my throat and become all business, addressing the task of helping him stretch his amputated leg. Without hesitating, I lift it and place both hands on the back of his up-stretched stump. His nostrils flare at my touch this time.

"You don't have to . . ." he protests.

"You ready?" I press against the back of his thigh as I look forward, out the window. He doesn't wrap his arms around me this time, but I count to twenty before releasing him.

Looking at my shoulder, he says, "Thank you."

"No problem."

When I try to hold him in a cradle stretch, the ridiculousness of my slender arms straining to gather around the bulk of his curled-up body makes us both smile. He hoists himself into position, but as soon as he relaxes into my hold he ends up lying on top of me. We make a few attempts, but finally find ourselves in a laughing tangle on the mat.

The rest of the room has grown quiet, and Pierce must realize it the same time I do. Leaning against each other, we look around and see everyone's attention aimed in our direction.

I spring up. "Um, did someone say some . . ." I trail off as everyone goes noisily back to what they were doing.

Pierce and I look at each other for a breath before he slides over and launches into a series of rapid sit-ups that are so intense it's like he's gone to another place in his head.

I think about what might have been between us if everything were completely different. If we were each whole. Pierce would probably still be on the other side of the globe. And Jay and I might be biking together, chasing down a fresh breeze. Or maybe kissing Jay would've been a onetime thing.

I sigh and lie down on the mat beside Pierce. Join him in doing enough sit-ups to block out everything except my burning stomach muscles and how much I want to stop.

13

By the time I'm limping toward Mom's car my abdominal muscles are so cramped I can barely stand. Despite the pain, my endorphins are kicking, since after sit-ups Pierce and I hit the exercycles hard.

Climbing into the car, I catch a glimpse of him stepping into the woods.

"Who was that?" Mom points through the window to where Pierce disappeared.

I shrug and will myself not to blush. "Just some guy who lost his leg in the war."

"Wow." She glances at me. "He was watching you. He looked away when he saw me looking, but he was definitely watching you."

I search for him through the trees but he's gone, and I wonder again how far he walks each day. Mom doesn't say anything more as she backs out of the Ulysses driveway and heads toward home.

"Jay should be at the house by the time we get there," I say, reestablishing my boyfriend's name and image in my mind.

"Good, your school supplies came today," she says. "Maybe you two can look them over together."

"He's going to help me with English and French." I think of how excited he was that I'm doing a unit on Shakespeare. "He's kind of awesome, huh?"

"Yes, he kind of is." Mom smiles.

My mind wings back to my body pressed against Pierce as we looked into each other's eyes.

Slouching down in my seat, I put in my earbuds. Sometimes, it's better to think about nothing.

That night after dinner, Dad announces, "Time to discuss this year's road trip." Before anyone can respond he turns to Mom. "Since Dyna has therapy and Harley has his . . . *job*, I was thinking you and I could take the Harleys." He smiles at her. "What do you say? Two weeks on the open road? It'll be like old times."

Mom frowns. "To be honest, I've been considering selling my bike. I just don't know what the kids would do if something happened to us."

Dad looks from Harley to me to Mom and says, "You're kidding, right? The kids are grown. You and I are expert riders. This trip will be us reclaiming our freedom."

"I just have an odd feeling and everyone knows that riding scared is a bad idea. Besides, we can't go away now." Mom gestures dramatically toward me. "Dyna is still recovering."

"*Dyna* is the most independent and capable girl I've ever met." Dad rises from the table. "If you're looking for an excuse not to go, fine. But don't act like Dyna needs you to sit around singing her lullabies."

"It's not an excuse. I'm just not ready to leave her alone."

"Alone?" Dad shoots. "She could never be alone with White-bread practically soldered to her side."

Mom stands in a huff, defending Jay, and the next thing I know the two of them are arguing about the trip full-throttle. Dad lays into her about acting like such a nervous wreck until Mom finally can't take it and starts screaming out in frustration every time he opens his mouth to speak.

"Listen, Beth—"

"Aaaaaaaa!"

"I'm just—"

"Aaaaaaaa!"

"I give—"

"Aaaaaaaa!"

For them it's like singing a romantic duet.

Mom has always said we come from a long line of passionate people and passionate people do not sit around discussing things calmly. They scream and holler at their loved ones and some-times throw endearingly small objects in their general direction. Harley and I quickly head out of the kitchen before Mom starts lobbing the plastic spice shakers again.

I prop myself up on the couch in the living room and loosen the straps to Son of Frankenfoot. Removing the brace, I try to ignore how scrawny my naked ankle looks as I feel for the plates and screws under my skin. *Freaky.* I trace my fingers along the scar that snakes partway up my shin. The scar from where my broken bone ripped through.

"Hey, your fall was what? Six weeks ago?" Harley must've been watching and sits down beside me. "If the two of them end up going, maybe you and I can spend a day on the mountain together."

I shake my head at him. "I'm not even close to being ready for the mountain."

"The last time I broke my tib I only took four weeks off." He smiles. "You have that brace of yours. I can top-rope you up the rock face in your harness."

"Thanks, bro. But I think I'll pass."

"Suit yourself, but trust me, it's best to get back out there as soon as possible. Those doctors are just overly cautious so they don't get sued."

"I think I'll take a chance listening to them, instead of my stoner brother."

"Ouch. That stings." He flicks me in the arm as he gets up to leave. "But I'm telling you, Dyna, you're ready."

By the next day my parents' flaming battle has burned down into a compromise. Mom will let Dad drag her away from me, but no way is he getting her onto a motorcycle. For road trips we usually take our old conversion van named The Fantastic Vandura, which is parked near the woods behind our house. Mom says it's Vandura or nothing.

Then she insists they delay their trip so she can go with me to my next doctor's appointment after therapy on Monday. There, I'm told I need to work a little harder at PT. As young, healthy, and active as I am, they expected me to be ready to move to an

Ace bandage by now. Instead, they want to see me again in two weeks. *I guess I should've done a few of those hateful toe-crunches after all.*

By the time we get back to the house Dad has already loaded Vandura for their trip. Harley's hanging out at the Ranch, but Dad has made him adjust his work schedule so he can drive me to and from therapy while they're gone. His exact words to Harley were, "It's the least you can do to take a little responsibility around this place."

Mom says goodbye, letting me know she'll come right back if I need her and warning me not to try to drive the car or do anything dangerous. She actually gets teary-eyed as she hugs me for the final time. Dad and I exchange glances over her shoulder and his look softens. I close my eyes and hug her back.

Mom drags the farewells out so long that Jay pulls into the driveway as we're still standing around. After giving him a soul-withering look, Dad climbs into Vandura's captain's chair and starts barking that they need to go, "Now, now, now, Beth!" He points to his chest. "You are poking the bear!" We all know he's about to rage, but Mom won't leave until she makes Jay promise to take care of me.

Of course he swears he won't let anything bad happen while she's gone.

Finally, Mom and Dad pull out with no plan beyond "heading west." The perfect vacation for them. Jay and I stand side by side on the deck waving as they back out of the driveway. Mom places her palm on the windshield, making it look like she's being abducted by Dad. Which, I suppose, she sort of is.

"Okay, looks like I'm in charge while Mom and Dad are away." Jay elbows me jokingly. I smile up at him for a beat before slipping inside the house. An unease seeps between us as we stand in the living room arm's-length apart. The quiet blasts the alarm that we're *alone, Alone, ALONE* and it feels like we should be heading straight to my bedroom.

Our make-out sessions haven't really come close to the big S.E.X. But Jay is the most serious boyfriend I've ever had and things have definitely been on an intercourse trajectory.

What the hell were Mom and Dad thinking leaving me home alone with my boyfriend? Maybe they just can't wait to be grandparents or something.

"You okay?" Jay is watching me and I notice he's inched closer.

I nod and lean over to grab the remote and flip on the television. We sit down on the couch together, but he must sense the change in dynamic with no supervision, real or imagined. He plays with his earlobe nervously, and I release the Velcro straps on Son of Frankenfoot before realizing this may be misinterpreted as some sort of kinky erotic foreplay.

"Ankle's sore," I explain. "The doctor was a little rough examining it." Jay springs up to ease my brace off and give me a massage. He's extra-gentle with my exposed scars, not wanting to rub too close to where the damage is worst. When his hands begin to work their way up to my thigh I tense, and he drops back down to the portion of my leg that's actually been injured. He mentions taking me to eat at my favorite bistro later as he expertly kneads the arch of my foot. It feels so good I close my eyes and let out a groan. His hands freeze.

Opening my eyes I see him smirking at me and realize my moans sound a little too much like "Dyna's porno sound track." "Sorry." I blush.

He laughs as he continues massaging. "I understand you've been through a lot, Dyna." He leans in closer. "I will absolutely wait until you're ready for us to be intimate. And then probably wait beyond that because I don't want to spoil what we have." His eyes search my face. "But if you keep making those noises I'm going to have to go upstairs and take a cold shower."

I clamp my lips shut in a display of chastity that makes him laugh. It's as if he just read my mind and put all my fears to rest. There couldn't be a more perfect guy to be with for my first time. Tender, caring, gentle. I reach up and caress the side of his smooth face a moment before leaning back on the couch.

"Maybe I'll talk to my mom about going on the pill soon." I hold my breath waiting for his reaction.

He looks at me and frowns. "One of my sisters got really depressed when she was on the pill," he says. "It was awful. Plus, it increases chances of blood clots. Dyna, your body has been through so much trauma. I wouldn't feel right about it."

"Well, I don't think they make a pill for guys and I can't trust a condom on its own." I think about the way one small defect in a flimsy rubber membrane could screw up my whole life, and I realize something. I sit up. "Hey, wait a minute. Did you bring one with you?" I accuse.

"What?" Jay's green eyes are wide.

"A condom." I reach over and start digging at his jean pockets. "Did you bring protection?"

"Dyna." He tries to stop my hands. "Come on. I wouldn't do that."

"You had to consider the possibility, Jay. I mean, come on. Parents out of town. Place to ourselves."

"Okay, yes, as a matter of fact I did think of it. And that's why I purposely didn't buy anything. I figured if things got out of control, taking a drive to RiteAid would slow us down. Give us a chance to get our heads on straight." He rubs my arm. "We've only been together a little over six weeks, and that's if we count the ambulance ride as our first date."

"Oh, that totally counts," I tease, starting to relax again. "I just don't want you to have the wrong idea about me. Despite my mad skills at dirty-word Scrabble, it just so happens I'm a virgin."

I try not to be hurt when Jay isn't able to cover his surprise.

I really can't blame him. He didn't know much about me beyond my wild reputation when we started hanging out. And it feels good to have such an open discussion about our boundaries, rather than the typical grope-fest that usually goes on until I have to get firm with a guy and shut him down. This feels like the most healthy, mature relationship I could ever imagine.

And I'm happy knowing Jay will be my first. *Now it's just a matter of when.*

14

Harley has been having fun teasing me about the way I constantly grab at the hand rest as he flies like a demon to and from Ulysses with the doors off his Jeep. Still, I'm not even a little bit surprised when I walk out of the center on Thursday and discover he isn't waiting for me. He probably tried to squeeze in a little skydiving since the weather is gorgeous. I'm left standing alone like a loser in the middle of the parking lot.

"Good workout today," Pierce says from behind me. I turn around and smile. The two of us got into yet another competition, and with my ankle brace wrapped tight I was able to hold a steady 60 RPMs on the exercycle. I'm still a little high from it.

He asks, "Where's your ride?"

I check my phone, but it's just as clueless as I am. "My folks are away and my big brother isn't exactly super-reliable." Leaning on my birchwood cane, I do a few deep knee bends so I don't stiffen up.

Pierce offers, "You're welcome to wait at my house. I'm right through the woods."

I falter before deciding. "Sure, I'll just text my brother a message to pick me up there. What's the address?"

After all, I have been wondering how far the walk is to his house. But if this is so completely innocent my heart probably shouldn't be beating quite this hard.

Despite their unevenness, our footsteps are quiet as I follow Pierce along the twisting trail. I breathe in the rich scent of things growing and things decomposing and I smile up at the tangled leaves woven into an archway overhead. I have always adored trees from every angle, but this is my favorite.

The undersides of trees.

I am connected to something greater.

I've stopped walking and pull my attention from above to find Pierce watching me. I feel exposed.

"Just looking at the trees," I say, tracing a root with my cane.

He nods and looks up. "I get it."

We start moving forward again, and after about ten minutes we enter a clearing of high grass that leads to the cropped back-yard of a stone house. We're greeted at the tree line by a wire-haired beige mutt lurching awkwardly toward us through the tall grass. I can't figure out what's happening to make the dog flail back and forth like that.

Then I see and swing to face Pierce. "You have a three-legged dog?"

His grin is wide and genuine. "This is Anders." He grabs the mutt behind both ears and playfully ruffles his head. When he lets go, the dog limps to me and nuzzles his nose deep into my crotch.

Pierce scolds, "Anders!" as I stagger. He grabs the dog's collar and drags him out of my personal space. "Sorry about that."

I laugh. "Where'd you get the name Anders?"

"'The Steadfast Tin Soldier.' By Hans Christian Andersen."

I nod, trying to remember the story and thinking it has something to do with toys.

"My mom was on my case to get a helper dog after she read some article about soldiers committing suicide. I'm sure she imagined some nice golden retriever keeping me from offing myself after Afghanistan."

"It is *really* hard to be sad around golden retrievers."

Pierce laughs. "Yeah, well, instead of going to the pet store I headed straight to the pound, and as soon as I saw him I knew he was the one." Pierce rakes his fingers down Anders's back. "I was still getting used to my missing leg at the time, and he seemed totally cool with his."

I reach down to pet Anders and he immediately flips to his back as if to ask, "But have you seen my belly?" I laugh. "He does seem to have a great outlook."

We scratch Anders's belly together for a moment before heading to the house. As we reach it the back door swings open and a thin woman steps out wiping her hands on her jeans. "How was therapy?" she calls before looking up. "Oh, I'm sorry. Hello. I'm Eva, Pierce's mother."

Pierce steps between us. "Hey, Mom, this is Dyna. Her brother's late to pick her up from Ulysses so I said she could wait here."

"Of course." She gives me a smile, but it doesn't reach her eyes until she turns them back to Pierce. "Do you want some lunch?"

"We're fine, Mom," he says, as he leads me into the house.

In the living room I spot a framed photo of Pierce wearing a dark blue uniform. His peaked service hat is pulled down to his eyebrows and there's a spark in his eyes that makes me wonder if it was a cute girl taking his picture. And if maybe he was flirting with her. The Pierce I know looks haunted by comparison.

He tells his mom we're going to wait in his room and gives her a swift kiss on the temple before heading down a hallway.

"Nice to meet you," I say, feeling graceless as she watches me lurch after the limping boy and dog.

Once we're in his room, Anders heads straight for a doggie bed in the corner and wraps himself into a circle. Shutting the door, Pierce tells me, "My mom's cool, but she would interrogate you into the ground given the chance." He smiles. "She's a little protective since I got home."

"Oh, I know how that feels. My mom barely let me out of her sight for weeks after my accident."

Pierce's room is sparsely decorated and I don't see any sign of his Purple Heart medal. In fact, the only award certificate displayed has gold lettering over an iridescent blue butterfly. "Let me guess." I point to it. "Ulysses?"

He laughs. "I came back home seriously messed up and that place helped save me. I still keep in touch with most of the folks from my first group."

He points to his dresser where a group shot of mismatched people sits beside a bigger picture showing a platoon of men wearing Army fatigues. A cigarette points from the corner of Pierce's smiling lips in the Army photo, and instead of remembering everything I know about lung cancer and emphysema and how disgusting smoking smells, all I can think is, *Damn, he's sexy.*

I ask, "No girlfriend photos?" It's exactly the type of comment I would've made to a guy before my accident, but now it surprises me so much I nearly clap my hands over my mouth.

"Ironic," Pierce says. "My last relationship was basically with photos of a girl." He settles himself on his bed and gestures for me to join him.

I sit down near the pillows. "So, were these photos you were dating *special* photographs?"

He laughs. "Oh, the girl was real." He swings his leg up onto the bed and starts stretching as he casually tells me about the girlfriend he hooked up with a few weeks before he was deployed. He explains how being separated so dramatically just made everything more intense and romantic. Pausing to look out the window, he says, "Being in Afghanistan was nothing like I expected, and I found myself clinging to the hope of this girl. Reading her love letters and staring at her photos. Imagining our reunion." He shakes his head. "In my mind she became more than one person could ever actually be."

He twists his torso back and forth before going on. "She was obviously upset when I came home all busted up and wrecked in the head, but we still really wanted to make things work between us. Except here's the thing." He looks at me. "I was completely knocked out by how unremarkable she was. And I don't mean she wasn't pretty either. If anything she looked even better than I'd remembered."

I squint at the bright light streaming in the window, and at his honesty.

"She just seemed happy enough waiting on tables and partying every night. Sleepwalking her way through life. She never had much to say beyond how much she loved me. When I gave her back her letters and photos we were both devastated." He rubs his hands together slowly. "But there was no way I could ever get past her being unremarkable."

The way he looks at me makes me wonder if he thinks I could be remarkable.

I want to be remarkable.

There's a soft knock on the door and Pierce's mom calls, "Care for some strawberry lemonade?" He glances at the ceiling as if he's annoyed but springs from the bed right away to let her in.

"Sorry to interrupt, but I thought the two of you could use a little snack." She sets a round tray filled with shortbread cookies and two pink drinks on Pierce's nightstand.

"Thanks, Mom." He gives her an almost imperceptible shrug. She looks at me.

"Hope your therapy is going well," she says. "Isn't the Ulysses Center great?"

"Yeah, my mom loves it, too," I answer, and she rewards me with a light chuckle.

"Watching our children suffer is the hardest thing a parent can go through." She ruffles her hand through Pierce's hair and he doesn't stop her. "I hope your mom is doing okay."

I think of Dad dragging her on their road trip and answer honestly. "She's getting better."

"Okay, Mom," Pierce says. "Thanks for the drinks."

"Sorry, I'll go." She turns by the door and pinches lightly at the outer seam of her jeans. "Please let your mom know I'll be happy to listen if she needs to talk."

I look at her standard-issue tank top and imagine her reaction to my tattooed mother. The funny thing is, there's something about her that makes me think they might get along. She closes the door behind her, leaving Pierce and me to silently devour the cookies and lemonade.

I sit back, allowing shortbread to dissolve on my tongue as I think of him sleeping in the desert with photos of an undeserving girl underneath his pillow.

Swallowing, I launch into the story of the time I was hanging on a cliff early one morning when a prop plane buzzed by close enough for the pilot to wave hello. Pierce listens intently as I share my most impressive hiking, biking, and climbing adventures. I even tell him about my crazy tattooed biker parents and my brother who's the smartest stoner anyone could ever meet. When the subject turns to bouldering I discover Pierce is familiar with some of the best spots.

"Sounds like you've got some serious work to do to get your butt back out there," he says.

My insides lie down on the floor. "I can't do any of that stuff anymore."

"You're kidding, right?" He laughs. "Dyna, you can't quit on a part of who you are. *I'm* planning to do most of the stuff you're talking about. You can't let anything keep you from what you love."

I mumble, "What I love."

"It's obvious, the way you light up when you talk about the

Gunks. You're meant to be on those mountains. Your love for adventure is contagious."

Our eyes lock, and we both lean forward. He brushes the cookie crumbs off his mouth and chin with one slow swipe of his palm, and I just stare at those beautiful lips. I want him to kiss me so much I realize I'm wiggling my fingers behind my back, but I know this isn't right.

"I have a boyfriend," I say, expecting him to fall back at this news.

Instead he moves even closer. He's near enough for me to feel his warm breath when he says, "You mean that pretty boy who drives you sometimes?"

"Jay is supersmart and he's really, really good to me." I turn my gaze out the window. "He saved my life."

Pierce reaches up, drawing my hair back as he whispers in my ear, "But is he remarkable, Dyna?" He slides his warm palms onto either side of my face and I look at him.

I imagined his soldierly sense of honor keeping things controlled, but his lips dip to that heady, unmistakable angle. *This is too dangerous.* I panic. "You don't seem the type to kiss someone else's girlfriend."

"I'm really not all that nice a guy." His words send my pulse into my throat.

Pierce caresses the sides of my face with his thumbs as he moves closer. *Oh, shit.* I close my eyes.

My nerve endings pound and my heart flails.

But my lips stay bare.

Opening my eyes I see him holding back, watching my mouth

as his jaw flexes. He *is* that nice a guy after all. His gaze stays clicked in, but he shifts away from me and lets his hand drop to my thigh, where it burns.

I try to envision Jay's face, imagine a boyfriend-powered energy shield,

but the momentum is too much and Pierce

pulls at me

like the gravity that dragged me off the rails.

I can't hold on anymore.

In one smooth motion I lunge forward, grab both sides of his neck, and seal my lips to his. The force of my lunge pushes him backward, but when he eases down on the bed it's slow and deliberate and he carries me with him. I'm vaguely impressed by his abdominal strength as I

Feel him.

Kiss him.

Taste him.

Boy mixed with cookies. *My new favorite flavor.*

He kisses me back.

Gently at first, then with

greater intensity.

His arms wrap around me and

my whole body responds and I know I'm a goner. I've just dropped off a cliff and am falling and . . .

"Pierce?" There's a knock at the door and we roll apart but keep our foreheads pressed together.

Pierce is breathing heavily, but his voice sounds normal as he answers, "What is it, Mom?"

"Dyna's brother is here."

Pierce sits up and runs his hand through his hair, making a tuft of it stick up. I want to keep kissing him so much I could weep. He calls to his mother, "We'll be right out." Standing, he asks if I'm okay.

"You mean besides being a terrible girlfriend?" I look at him with my lips pursed and resist the urge to reach for him again.

"That was my fault," he says.

"Right. Your fault I gave you an attack kiss."

His laugh is pained. "I think I made you do it. I wanted it so bad." He runs his fingers through his hair again, making it lie smooth this time. "I don't know what this is." He points from me to himself. "But don't count on me being strong enough to resist you."

He leans down and whispers into my ear, "Dyna. You. Are. *Remarkable.*"

Somehow I manage to get both of my legs working, find my cane, and give Anders a pat goodbye. Forcing one step after the other, I head down the hallway to meet Harley.

Except that Pierce's mom was wrong.

My brother didn't come to pick me up.

My boyfriend did.

15

Sitting beside Jay on the drive home, I watch him from the corner of my eye as my mind shorts out on what the hell I should do.

I don't deserve this great guy. I picture the way he reacted when Pierce and I emerged from his bedroom, both of us blushing and rumpled.

Jay introduced himself as a writer and said to Pierce, "I noticed that the article in the *New Paltz Times* didn't have any direct quotes about your experience in Afghanistan. In fact, I couldn't find any interviews with you at all and I'd like to help you get your story out there."

"Thanks, but I don't really need my story *out there*," Pierce responded, gesturing vaguely toward the windows.

"Your heroism deserves national attention. Who knows where the right article could take you?" Jay looked to me for confirmation, but I kept dropping eye contact with everyone.

Pierce repeated he'd rather not be interviewed, but Jay insisted. "Do you realize how rare it is to find an honest-to-god hero? People need to hear about it."

Pierce's eyes flashed hotly and he said through his teeth, "I don't need people getting ideas about me being some kind of hero. I'm not."

His mother put a hand on one of his shoulders and he let them both droop as she told Jay, "I'm sorry, but this interview isn't going to happen." Looking at her son with a mixture of pride and sadness, she said, "I agree he's a hero, but Pierce just wants to move on. I'm sure your sister's ready to get home by now."

"My sis . . . ?" Jay gave a confused look.

"Thank you for the cookies," I mumbled, and bolted for the door. Jay apologized for being pushy and then insisted on giving Pierce his phone number and e-mail before we left.

I tune back in to him talking about how great an interview would be as we drive through the woods toward my house. "This one inspirational story could put me right on the map," he says.

It's the same tunnel focus that must've made him miss the combination of anger and want in Pierce's blue eyes as we left. I cringe all over again at the image of Anders standing alone on the front porch wagging his tail as he watched us pull away, not understanding that I'd just betrayed everyone.

I mentally shove all my feelings into the glove box in front of me and lock them away.

Jay grins. "Now you just have to convince Pierce he can trust me." The word "trust" is a grenade in my chest.

"I don't think trust is the issue," I say. "He just doesn't want the attention."

"That's silly. Who wouldn't want to be labeled a hero?"

My mind goes back to Pierce's bedroom, and once again I'm with him making out, losing control . . .

the glove box pops open and a tangle of feelings dumps into my lap.

I need to get myself reined in.

That kiss was too wild.

Pierce is too fucked up and I'm too damaged.

We'd just go down in flames.

And besides,

Jay is everything to me.

Looking at his handsome profile, I'm comforted by a wave of familiarity. Even riding along this twisting stretch of road, I feel safe. It's pretty much the opposite of how I felt this morning riding with my brother. I remember the pavement flying by so close to my busted-up foot as we careened around the windy road to Ulysses.

I clutch Jay's hand. "What happened to Harley?"

"What do you think happened?" He gestures to the clear sky.

I groan. "Figures."

"He texted me when he got your message. I was at the pool with my sisters, but I got here as fast as I could."

"Thank you so much for this."

"Don't worry about it," Jay says. "I've got you." He presses the palm of my hand to his lips and I notice that tiny scar on his right dimple. He is saving me all over again.

I can keep pretending nothing happened.

I can't lose him.

Pretend nothing happened.
It would actually be pretty selfish of me to hurt
him with the truth.
Nothing
happened.

16

By the time my parents are almost finished with their road trip I've skipped more than a week of therapy sessions, and the answering machine is filled with long-winded messages from Miss explaining why I need to get back to the Ulysses Center immediately. Or at least it would be filled if I wasn't deleting all her messages.

Right now she's leaving one chastising me for missing Frank's recovery assignment. It's the Friday before Labor Day weekend, and apparently he successfully drove the whole group up and down the mountainside switchbacks in the Ulysses van late last night.

Harley and Jay are sitting on the living room floor across from me, and Harley laughs hysterically as Miss's imploring voice drones on. "You are not just letting yourself down, Dyna. You are letting the entire group down as well. You have a responsibility . . ."

I stand up, walk over to the machine, and click off the speaker so Miss can leave the rest of her guilt-heaping message in silence. Harley coughs as he passes his joint to Jay.

Moving back to my spot on the floor, I grumble, "As if I'm a terrible person because I didn't feel like getting tossed around the back of some stupid van until I puked." I try not to picture the smile that must've been on Frank's round face after he accomplished his assignment.

"Dyna." Jay pauses a moment for a quick draw before passing the joint to me. "Have you thought about what you're going to tell your mom?"

I shake my head and hand Harley his joint without taking a drag. "I still have a few days before they get home. I'll come up with something." At first Jay tried to talk me into going back to Ulysses, but I wouldn't budge. He holds up both palms in surrender now, clearly not wanting to debate this with me again.

In fact, judging by his lopsided grin and glassy eyes, he doesn't want to do much of anything. *He should try taking the SATs now.* I laugh at the image of him just coloring in random circles with his #2 pencil. Maybe connecting the dots to make a picture of Mickey Mouse. Jay joins me in laughter, which makes me laugh even harder.

"Thanks a bunch for getting my boyfriend stoned." I shove Harley and he falls over, laughing.

"You can thank my buddy for getting me this primo shit." Harley straightens and holds up the last bit of joint as if it were a sacred object. The front door slams shut behind us.

"Shit!" Harley drops the burning roach and scrambles to get it off the carpet before it burns a hole. "Shit, shit, shit."

"Oh, please." Dad's booming voice nails us all to the floor. "Don't stop what you're doing on our account."

He and Mom are standing in the doorway. Mom looks from Harley to Jay to me with her mouth half opened. She seems to be deciding which of us she's the most shocked at.

Dad does not suffer from her indecision. "Harley! Dyna! Get to your rooms. Now! And Jay?" With a voice so calm it is utterly terrifying, he says, "Please leave."

He doesn't need to repeat himself.

Harley and I text back and forth from the shelter of our bedrooms. The force of Mom and Dad's joined anger can be heard like a hurricane forming in our living room. Harley writes:

How bout we blame jay for the doob?

I write back:

NO WAY! Dad would kill him!

But would save us. Jay can be hero. **Harley**

Dead hero. **Me**

Just heard dad say they should kick me out. **Harley**

I heard too. Sucks for you. **Me**

Thanks a bunch. **Harley**

Sorry. **Me**

A text from Jay makes my phone buzz again.

I was too afraid to drive stoned. I'm parked around the corner. What's going on?

Mister Responsible.

Do NOT come back here. **Me**

Not EVER? **Jay**

No Silly. They're mostly pissed at Harley. **Me**

I hope he doesn't try to blame the joint on me. Jay

He wouldn't do that. Me

Sorry. I'm glad Harley and I are cool. Jay

R U sure they won't believe it was jays joint? Harley

I hear the message machine beep on in the living room and Miss's recorded voice streams up through the heating vent. With a jolt I scamper awkwardly down the stairs to stop my parents from listening to the whole message. I arrive too late, and Mom and Dad turn to look at me standing in the middle of the living room just as the recording ends. All at once I'm seeing them the way the rest of the world must see them. As a scary-looking couple covered in tattoos who may or may not be about to rip my head off. Instinctively, I fake a pain in my leg and fall to the couch, hoping to elicit some pity from Mom.

"Dyna, we need to talk." I can tell from her tone that pity is not the emotion she's feeling. At all.

Dad calls for Harley to come down, and he joins me on the couch.

We both keep our heads bowed.

Harley's punishment is that he is simultaneously kicked out and grounded. Actually, he's given one month to figure out some sort of plan before he has to move out, but in the meantime he's stuck at home when he's not working.

"Everything makes sense now," Dad says to him gruffly. "Explains why you've been acting more and more like a damn pothead. Because you *are* a damn pothead. I'm very disappointed in you, son."

Harley has never looked more sober.

"And you, little miss." Dad turns to me and I try to explain that I wasn't smoking.

He cuts me off. "I know it was Harley's weed. I still want to ban you from ever seeing Whitebread again."

I tense my shoulders at the thought. "You can't—"

"But . . ." Dad says. *Oh, how I love the sound of that "but."* "Your mom is convinced he's worth another chance."

"Let Jay know he's on notice," Mom says sharply. "Clearly, I need to get more involved in your life. Did you even start looking over your homeschool lessons yet?"

My chin rests on my chest. "No."

Mom's words press together. "And I can't believe you just *stopped* going to therapy."

I cringe. "Please, Mom. You can't make me go back there."

"Can. Too." She gives me a steady gaze that tells me Ulysses is happening.

So now I'll have to go back and face all the people I've been letting down. I just hope Pierce has forgotten about that kiss, because despite everything, when I close my eyes

I can still feel it.

17

When Jay and I lean across the seat to kiss goodbye that Tuesday morning, I swing my eyes to the windshield just in time to see Pierce move into view. He's watching us. *Shit.*

Jay insisted on driving me since school starts tomorrow and he won't be able to drop me off anymore. He did manage to change his free period so he can pick me up on days he doesn't have newspaper. He tips his chin toward Pierce when he sees him.

"You can let your friend know he's off the hook," Jay says, and my blood begins to rush. "I scored an interview with a woman in town who gave birth after surviving cancer in one of her ovaries."

"That's great," I croak drily.

"It's not exactly the war hero story I wanted, but a miracle baby is something I can definitely work with."

I slink out of the car and head toward the deck, careful not to catch up to the one-legged boy who must loathe me by now.

When Jay showed up at my house this morning at nine-thirty, my dad and I were sitting at the kitchen table together in silence. Dad was sketching a wicked heart tattoo, and I was getting overwhelmed reading through my homeschooling assignments. It's one thing to take high school one dreary day at a time. It is something else entirely to see a year's worth of work as one massive, impossible mountain. It didn't help that Dad never even asked if I wanted eggs for breakfast. And I really did.

Jay walked in the door, apology first, and Dad surprised me by acting civilized toward him. "Maybe I underestimated you," Dad said. "It took guts to come back here and face me head-on after what happened."

Jay looked at me as if to ask, "Should I be afraid?"

I shook my head no. It seems my boyfriend has finally displayed sufficient backbone and character, not to mention *balls*, to earn my father's respect.

I slowly climb the stairway toward my moment of dread and remember that first meeting when I could barely make it to the top. It's a little more of a struggle than it was the last time I was here. Still, I run out of steps too soon and stand leaning against my cane in front of the group. Miss and Frank are the only ones willing to make eye contact.

Clearing my throat, I squeak, "So, what did I miss?"

Even Frank looks away. I slump into the last free chair between Pierce and Miss, drop my cane to the floor, and stare at my knees. I wonder if they've kept an empty chair in the circle this whole time.

Miss welcomes me back stiffly and has the group launch into a recap. I'm surprised by how much I've missed. Besides Frank's victorious Van Driving Odyssey, he's scheduled for a big speaking gig at New Paltz High School warning about the dangers of texting and driving.

"I'm nervous, but excited," he says.

Sparky reassures him he's going to kill it and goes on to report that his arms are getting much stronger. He even managed to plant some late-season spinach and radishes over the weekend. Polly sounds like she's finally over her ex and enjoying being single for the first time since she hit puberty.

I get the sense that the group has grown past me. Especially when Miss announces that Pierce got a new prosthetic attachment so he can start running.

"He plans to enter this year's Turkey Trot 5K," she says proudly. I turn toward him in amazement.

He won't look at me.

Rita pushes her braids back and gives a loud sigh. "Well, I suppose it's time."

Her tone is grave, and I figure she's about to start harping about

Badass Bitch Power or our Lord Jesus Christ or something.

But she only wants to

let us know she

has cancer with a capital *C* and she is

sorry she kept it a secret and the

prognosis is bad although she's okay with the fact

that she's dying.

My mouth goes dry and I look to Pierce. He's nodding sadly. *He already knew.* Based on reactions I can see this is news for the rest of the group. That is, aside from Miss, who looks more proud of Rita than upset.

"I beat breast cancer when I was younger," Rita says. "Bet you all wondered why I've got such perky ta-tas for an old-timer." She juts out her chest. "They're falsies." We remain mute and she goes on, "I almost died thirty years ago. A huge chunk of my life has been bonus time." She looks around slowly. "I cannot be anything but grateful."

At this, Polly lunges to kneel in front of her, puts her face in the older woman's lap, and hugs her around the waist. "There, now." Rita strokes Polly's smooth hair. "I'm not dying today." Frank releases tears as big as my fist and Sparky rubs his arms, his usually serene face imprinted with sorrow.

Rita's not getting chemo since the cancer's too far along in her pancreas. She doesn't want to spend her final months bald and in agony and in a hospital bed. She reaches down, gently tips Polly's face up, and looks her in the eye. "I'm planning to stretch things out a bit." Rita winks. "The doctors are giving me until midwinter, but you bitches better believe I'll be here to watch spring unfold."

I can't even begin to process the thought of Rita dying of cancer. My heart clenches at how frail she looks all of a sudden.

"I've had such a blessed life," she says. "I know where I'm going and it's a wondrous place. I am not afraid."

The next half hour drags by more slowly than my whole first day did, as we're each encouraged to unpack our unbearable feelings about Rita's horrible news.

Pierce is careful not to look at me the whole time, which is better than him hopping up and confronting me. So I return the favor of silence when we all move darkly to physical therapy. He and I do our stretches side by side without a word or touch.

Workout Barbie doesn't interfere and only Rita glances our way once or twice.

When we climb on the exercise bikes, I'm surprised at how much my time away has set me back. I halfheartedly pedal along with my ankle brace, but my pace and breathing are all off and I need to keep stopping. When my foot slips and the pedal bangs my shin I curse under my breath.

Out of the corner of my eye I catch Pierce smiling slightly at that as he pedals smoothly along.

And I feel how much riding an exercycle

is really just making wheels spin.

"Argh!" I fling *Romeo and Juliet* onto the floor. Jay is sitting beside me on the couch and looks up from his tablet.

"Trouble with the Bard?" He smiles.

"I doth need a friggin' break." We've been doing schoolwork for the past few hours, and even though we're only a week into it I'm already starting to fall behind. Skipping "just one subject" each day adds up fast. I reach over and pinch Jay's ear playfully. "Want to go for a walk?"

I've been trying to exercise more, and I got the green light to switch up Son of Frankenfoot with an Ace bandage and cane whenever I feel comfortable.

Jay glances out the window and wrinkles his nose. "It's getting dark."

"I miss being in the woods. Under the stars . . ."

His face lights up. "I have just the thing." He taps at the

screen of his tablet for a moment and then holds it up toward the ceiling with the display facing us. "Check out this cool app I found."

I'm confused for a second. The screen is black, but it's speckled with white lights that look like "Stars?" They stay in place as he moves the tablet around and it's as if he's holding an X-ray screen that shows the whole wide sky with the stars all around us.

He grins at my look of amazement and shifts so I can lie back against him. He slowly aims the tablet around the room and the names of various constellations light up.

"See, there's Aries." A white outline of a goat appears, connecting a cluster of stars.

"I've always hated that constellation crap," I say. "Those stars look nothing like a goat without the drawing."

"It's not a goat, it's a ram." Jay laughs. "And that's part of what's so cool about it. Someone in ancient times looked up at the stars and saw a ram and managed to convince everyone else to see a ram, too."

He slides the tablet around and reads the names of other stars as they appear. "Hey, Naos. Wazzup, Algenib?" And then he zeroes in on stars that are just a series of letters and numbers. "What happened, NGC1039? No love?"

I laugh as Jay readjusts his angle on the couch. He places the tablet faceup on his chest. "There. Can you see what that says?"

I lean over the screen, which now shows a large compass rose with arrows pointing to the north, south, east, and west. The long spire that's pointing directly at Jay's grinning face reads "True North."

I pay him with a kiss. "Okay, that is definitely the sweetest, geekiest thing I've ever seen." I take the tablet and hold it up as I lie back against his chest,

listening to his strong,

steady

heartbeat

as the two of us gaze at the stars together.

The temperature drops the following week as summer releases us to mid-September's hold. Of course, Miss insists we continue to sit outside. She put plastic guards around the bird feeders to stop the squirrels from ransacking them, so Rita has been bringing bread from home to feed them. The squirrels are getting alarmingly fat.

The topic for today is faith, and when Miss asks Pierce to begin the sharing his blue eyes sweep around to everyone except me. He says he was having a really bad day a couple of weeks ago and went out to sit on the porch where he's always enjoyed looking at the Catskill Mountains.

He gestures toward them. "The mountains were completely fogged in that day and I was kind of pissed. I mean, can't a guy at least enjoy the view when he's feeling like shit?" Miss laughs uncomfortably.

"But here's what I realized. I knew those mountains were still there. I could sense them standing strong and solid behind the fog." He looks around, avoiding me again. "And I realized that's exactly what faith is. Being sure of something, even when we can't see it."

Pierce glances at me for a microsecond and looks away. I feel like he just shot me.

"Oh, Pierce!" Miss is in ecstasy and Rita and Sparky can't help but applaud.

When it's my turn to share I counter Pierce by explaining how sometimes faith means finding other people we can trust enough to lean on. I describe the ways my *boyfriend* has been there for me throughout my whole recovery. "I have faith in him," I say, and Pierce just stares at the air in front of his face the whole time I'm talking.

Polly tells me I'm nuts and makes an inspiring declaration about having faith in herself. "I know who I am and I don't need a guy to make me feel complete."

Rita flings her arms in the air in victory and kisses Polly on both cheeks, but at least I made my point with Pierce.

I know I totally wrecked things between us. There's no way to go back to being friends after a kiss like that. But it's really important that I remind us both in as many ways and as often as possible that I have a boyfriend.

Pierce needs to know I'm finished playing with fire.

Subject closed. New topic.

18

The following week my birthday falls on a Tuesday, and despite Jay's willingness to ditch school to spend the whole day with me, Mom insists I can't miss another session at Ulysses. Besides, Miss needs to fulfill her eccentric duty by celebrating my special day with a god-awful-sounding drum circle out on the deck. It's another charming Ulysses "tradition."

That evening, Jay gives me a plethora of wildflowers and takes me out for sushi and a romantic comedy. When the movie's over, he guides me with my cane to a nearby park. The playground is empty and I pump myself higher and higher on the swing until I'm light-headed. Jay recites a sonnet from the top of the jungle gym before taking me up the stairs of the elaborate wooden castle. He asks me to wait at the top while he runs to his car for something.

I grin when he comes back carrying a gift bag bursting with heaps of tissue paper. Stopping on the ground directly below me, he places his hand on his heart and calls up, " 'O, she doth teach the torches to burn bright!' "

"No more Shakespeare on my birthday," I yell down. "I want something original."

Laughing, he bounds up the stairs to me and holds out the gift bag. "Many trees gave their lives for this dazzling presentation."

"Lovely." I feel my smile widen.

Jay leans against the railing and pulls me to sit on the ledge beneath him. Clawing at the colorful paper, I uncover a chubby rainbow teddy bear with hearts for eyes.

"I know it's cheesy, but I saw him in Manny's front window and I couldn't resist," he says. Giving the bear a hug, I reach up to make it caress Jay's cheek until he laughs and leans down to kiss me.

Next I pull out a cover for my phone with the image of a star-filled sky on the back of it. "Since your phone is too ancient to get the stargazing app."

"Hey, I like my old phone." I smile as I look at the phone case. "This is seriously sweet. And I love that some couples may have a special song, but we have a geeky app."

"It will always be *our app*," Jay says.

Next I unwrap a retro silver bicycle bell that he attaches to my cane for me. "To get those *rotten kids* out of your way." I laugh as he pulls out my final gift and hands it to me. "And this is for after you get around to finishing *Romeo and Juliet*." It's a hardcover illustrated copy of Krakauer's book *Into Thin Air*. "This one's about a group of climbers who get stuck in a storm on Mount Everest."

"Wow, cool," I say, opening it to flip through the thick pages.

"Eight of them die."

I look at him. "Well, thanks for giving away the ending."

He chuckles. "Krakauer tells you that from the start. But it's amazing how quickly things can turn deadly when people don't respect nature's power. I mean, why would anyone even consider a crazy climb like that? I don't get it."

I stop at a full-page photo of Everest and trace my fingers over the craggy peak. The highest point on earth. "I do," I whisper.

"What?" Jay asks.

I smile and hold up the book. "Thank you. I love everything."

"Happy birthday, Dyna." He squeezes me. "Hope you don't mind that I didn't get you jewelry. I know you don't like wearing it."

"You got me there." I grin. "And anyway, wouldn't jewelry imply it's time for me to start putting out?"

Jay feigns shock and covers his mouth. "Dyna. What would make you think I'm ready to have sex with you?"

"We've been dating for almost three months." I stand, turn toward him, and give him the most luscious, seductive, tender kiss I can.

When I pull back, Jay pretends to almost collapse over the railing. "Is it too late to maybe swing by the jewelry store?"

I laugh. "Nice try." We look into each other's eyes and I add, "Maybe soon."

"Don't worry," he says. "We'll know when the time is perfect."

He's perfect. "We'll know," I agree, and pull him down so we're completely hidden by the walls of the castle.

He stretches out beside me in the shadows and I breathe in

the familiar scent of his shampoo. Putting my hand on his chest I say, "I love you, Jay."

His eyes widen and he caresses my cheek. "Wow, do I ever love you, too," he says, and moves in to seal it with a perfect spearmint kiss.

19

Workout Barbie is super-rah-rah-psyched about my progress that Friday. "I spoke with your doctor and ankle fusion is definitely not necessary." She grasps my unwrapped foot and painfully tests my ankle rolls. "In fact, I think we can get that range of motion where it needs to be." She takes me by the shoulders. "Dyna, with some extra pushing I believe you may eventually get full use."

Sparky is standing close by and calls out, "You hear that, guys? Dyna's getting her ankle back all the way."

"Eventually!" Barbie clarifies. "And with a *lot* of work."

Rita gives a "Hell yeah!" and the others begin to applaud.

"All right, okay." I hold up both my hands. "No need to go into another drum circle. *Please.*" But I can't keep the grin off my face.

The human Barbie has been pushing me to try the treadmill ever since I came back at the beginning of the month. It's almost October now, but I think I'm finally ready. Son of Frankenfoot is looking awfully worn and dirty, but I'm not quite ready to let the monster go.

Standing on the stopped belt, I take a few breaths before bumping the machine slowly up in increments until I hit 3.6 MPH. I keep it steady there until I catch my stride. Even though I'm not walking all that fast, I hold on to the front of the machine until Pierce passes by and points out that hanging on the bar cuts my workout effectiveness in half. He's wearing his running prosthetic, which looks like a large metal letter *J* from the side.

I let go and try to straighten out my uneven gait until I find a comfortable pace. The whir of another treadmill across from me starts up, and by the time I get my rhythm enough to look over, Pierce is already jogging smoothly along on it. I watch him run faster as he brings his machine up to a nice clip. With *one leg*.

I feel like my treadmill may as well be blinking "Begin Workout Now."

I poke my speed button four times, and then when that doesn't feel like much of an increase I give it two more. I'm at 4.2 MPH and now my long strides are hurried by the speed of the machine.

Any faster and I'll be jogging. A panicky feeling starts to rise in my chest as I fast-walk as quickly as I can. I look over at Pierce's focused expression. Watch him sweating.

I've drifted to the rear of the walking platform and realize I'm falling behind the treadmill's pace. I try to hurry my way back to where I can grab the front if I need to.

Son of Frankenfoot gives a strange stutter on the belt that throws off my stride.

I cry out as I'm pitched forward.

Pushing away panic, I have a split second to react.

My good ankle twists,

and I drop to the ground.

It's a good call. Letting myself fall is the best move for my ankle. Except that I'm on a treadmill and anything that falls on the moving belt gets dumped off the back end. Including me.

I grunt as my body does an awkward roll and I'm spit out onto the floor.

The dread washes over me and I am

curled in a ball,

helpless and broken all over again.

My eyes fill. *I knew this would happen.* I'm gutted by defeat. And then,

I get up.

And I am fine.

"Did you guys see that?" I laugh in disbelief through my tears as I rub my ankle and realize Pierce is right there. He must've rushed over as soon as he saw me falling. Was probably the one who hit the big red Stop button on my treadmill. But he didn't help me up or try to comfort me. He waited.

He's still breathing heavily from his run as he watches me swipe at my eyes and pull myself together. He asks if I'm sure I'm okay.

I look away and nod. And it's with mixed emotions that I climb back on that treadmill and try again.

20

I've entered Sunday afternoon TV-trance-zone on the couch when Dad walks in the door announcing, "Heads up! I've got a surprise guest!" Over the years he's done this thing where he'll randomly bring home clients he finds especially memorable or unique. Usually they're semi-famous musicians or superquirky artists who start out in his tattoo chair and end up at our dinner table. I look to the doorway.

Squinting at the silhouette beside my father, I see there's something familiar in the way the stranger is standing. The shadowed figure moves into the living room with the hint of a limp and I nearly scream in surprise.

"Hey, Dyna," Pierce says, "what're you doing here?"

"Um, I *live* here," I say, in such a way that I don't need to add, "And what the hell are you doing here?"

"Oh, wow." Pierce looks amused as he glances back and forth between my dad and me. "Yeah, I guess I can see a little resemblance."

I glare at him accusingly. "I look just like my mom."

"Hey, Dyna Glider," Dad says. "How do you know Private Pierce?"

"Pierce goes to Ulysses," I say tonelessly.

"The home of inside-out healing," Pierce confirms.

Dad smiles. "I just finished giving him an extraordinary tattoo."

I wish Jay was here to block the judgmental way Pierce is looking at me. As if curling up on a couch to watch reality television in the middle of the afternoon is some sort of crime or something. I sit up, flip the switch mid-bitch-fight, and try to look as if I haven't been in this same position for hours.

The silence in the wake of the dramatic onscreen shrieking stretches out awkwardly until Pierce breaks it. "Your dad sort of insisted I come and meet the family. It was a little cold, but that ride felt amazing."

"You mean you . . ."

"My first time on the back of a Harley." Pierce laughs. "I may need to get one of those."

I squint at Dad and try to picture him riding with Pierce's arms wrapped around his waist, his legs bent at uneven angles as they lean into the turns together.

"Pierce was just telling me about his adventures overseas." Dad claps him on the back. "I'm hoping some of his sense of honor rubs off on your brother."

I'm ready to escape the Pierce-worshipping party my dad is throwing here in our living room. Extracting myself from the couch, I stretch the stiffness out of my legs.

"Tell your mom I'm cooking up an early dinner and there's going to be an extra person at the table." He looks at Pierce. "Want to lend me a hand, soldier?"

Pierce gives me an apologetic shrug and the two of them head toward the kitchen. Best buddies in the world.

As I move to the stairs Dad calls after me, "Send your brother down to help us with the cooking."

I turn to give my dad an aggressive eye roll but catch Pierce's stare by accident. Dad's already in the kitchen, but Pierce is watching me go.

I feel the pull of him.

Breaking free, I make my way up the staircase but feel his blue eyes burning as I limp away. My heart pounds and I stop to catch my breath as soon as I'm out of view.

Finally, I hear Dad engage Pierce in a conversation about steak.

"Unghhh!" I stomp my good foot in rage.

I can't believe that the guy I've been trying to keep out of my head is staying for dinner.

"Dad's back to bringing random people home to feed," I tell Harley from the doorway of his bedroom. Nobody has brought up his eviction even though his month is up in a few days. He's playing his air guitar in front of the mirror now and turns to face me as he continues rocking out.

"Nice jamming," I say, "but you need to go help Dad cook."

Harley groans and I head to my room and close the door. *Mom would understand that Pierce is dangerous.* I picture her trying to mimic Dad's intimidation technique by lifting her dress and pointing to my birthdate tattooed on her belly. I imagine her asking Pierce aggressively, "Do you have any idea how precious my daughter is to me? Do you?" It would probably be pretty effective.

I take a moment to wrap my ankle tighter before reaching under my pillow and pulling out the poem Jay gave me earlier today. Unfolding the thick stationery, I smile as I reread the perfect words he wrote for me.

> *Love's herald fell from rusty sky*
> *Night Star craved wildflower's face*
> *True North did capture flower's sigh*
> *Finding fit in petal's embrace*

I have it memorized by the time Harley calls up to say the food is ready. Using my cane, I make my way downstairs and find everyone's already sitting around the table. The only open seat is next to Pierce, who's helping Dad serve up delicious-smelling skirt steaks with roasted asparagus and penne.

After we start eating Mom says, "I wasn't sure if Jay was joining us tonight." She glances at Pierce, and I realize I didn't need to say anything to her after all. Pierce doesn't flinch at the mention of Jay's name. In fact, he seems completely comfortable as we all noisily praise the tasty meal.

"I was just telling your dad how much I love this section of the woods," Pierce says. "Having the trail right behind the house must make it easy for you to get out and exercise. You bike, right, Dyna?"

"Ha!" Harley butts in before I can respond. "She hasn't been on her mountain bike since the day of her accident." I resist the urge to stick my tongue out at my big brother.

"What's up with that?" Pierce asks me. "I think *I* was back to biking sooner."

"I still can't believe you're a runner, too," Harley tells him. "You should totally do a triathlon or something."

"Except that I can only swim in circles now." Pierce laughs.

Harley says, "Man, that blows."

"Yeah, but to be honest I'm extremely lucky. I have buddies who came home in boxes." He looks at his hands.

"That's who the tat is for," Dad says. "It's four of his comrades' names written in sand and big ole sandy angel's wings on either side of them."

"It looks amazing," Pierce says.

Dad smiles proudly and the table is silent, as if my whole family is under the spell of Pierce's presence.

I blurt, "What about *Easy Rider*, Dad?" Everyone turns to look in my direction. "I thought you didn't believe in war. In fact . . ." Lunging over the table I pull up the right sleeve of Dad's T-shirt and reveal his peace-symbol tattoo that drips with the words "More Ink Less War." "Aha!" I accuse. "You and Mom still move Bush's autobiography into the crime section at bookstores."

"Dyna, we are not getting into a political debate," Mom says. "No arguing at the table."

I look at her. "Are you kidding me? The reason we *have* a table is so this family has a specific location to argue!"

"That's not why I brought Pierce into our home," Dad warns.

"It's fine," Pierce says. "I'm up for a discussion. Here, I'll even start us off. You know that saying 'It's a free country'?"

"Yeah." Dad looks wary.

Pierce levels him with his eyes. "Well, I love that saying."

This gets a rise out of my father, and with a "Listen here, I love this country just as much as anybody . . ." the two of them launch into a heated dispute over politics that instantly makes my head hurt.

". . . greatest nation . . ." ". . . foreign policy . . ." ". . . Taliban . . ." ". . . weapons of mass destruction . . ." ". . . defend the weak . . ." ". . . *cough* Iraq *cough* . . ."

"So much for polite conversation," Mom tells me as words ricochet around us. Harley is busy listening and interjecting lame comments that support both Pierce and Dad at different times.

When Dad's face hits a shade of red that suggests Pierce is seriously poking the bear, Mom yells out, "Okay, enough! This discussion is done. Subject closed! New topic!"

The two of them finally agree to disagree on ideology and aggressively finish their last bites of steak.

When Dad's face has returned to its natural color, he says, "Whatever my feelings on war, I do respect what you've done, soldier." To Harley and me he says, "I brought Pierce home to get you kids thinking about how you'll make your mark on this world."

"You know"—Harley runs his tongue over his lip ring—"to be honest I've always kind of imagined myself flying a plane."

"Here we go," Mom says. "We are not paying for flying lessons. We took enough of a hit when you washed out of culinary school."

There's an awkward pause, since everyone at the table knows Harley dropping out of cooking school is a sore spot. Everyone except for Pierce, that is, so he jumps right in. "You could learn to fly for free in the Air Force."

Mom and Dad both shift back in their seats, but Harley leans forward. "I never thought of that," he says.

Pierce describes the benefits of Air Force training, including the fact that once Harley's time is served he can become a private pilot and see the world. "You love being in the sky, might as well get paid for it."

It turns out that a person needs to be pretty smart and have good grades to get into the Air Force Academy and qualify for pilot training. But of course, that's not an issue for Harley.

His eyes sparkle, and I feel the need to extinguish all of this. "You'll have to lose the piercings, you know," I say, but Harley just shrugs. "And they do drug tests on pilots *all the time*."

"Not a problem." He grins at me and I can see he's serious. I look to Mom and Dad, but they seem equally lost for a way to make it clear that Harley cannot possibly join the Air Force.

Especially since, as Pierce is explaining, it seems that he certainly can.

"Hey, Pierce?" I pat him aggressively on the shoulder with the gauze that must still hurt from Dad's tattoo. "My brother's doing just fine without your *help*. Thanks."

Pierce doesn't flinch as he looks at me. "You told me he was a brilliant student who turned into a total pothead right after graduation."

Harley starts coughing loudly but I'm focused on Pierce. "He can't do this."

"You can't stop him," Pierce says. "I hate to break it to you, Dyna, but life is one giant risk. Stepping out and *trying* is the biggest risk a person can take, but it beats doing nothing."

I just stare at him.

"Sounds kind of like the family motto." Dad grins at Mom.

I stand up, pick up my plate, and start scraping the scraps into the garbage. "Mottos are stupid."

"Fine, but your brother's not." Pierce glares at me, and I resist the urge to stab him with my fork.

I clatter around the table, haltingly clearing the dishes. Pierce stands to bring his plate to me at the sink and I snatch it from him and lean in. "What makes you think you can just show up here and start messing with my family?"

"If I were here to mess with your family," Pierce says evenly, "I'd start with you. I'd tell you that accident didn't cripple you, Dyna. You're the one who did that to yourself."

"Now wait just one minute—" Mom says.

"I apologize," Pierce interrupts. "But I can't stand watching her hold so much back."

"You don't know anything about me," I shoot.

He locks in his gaze. "I know you possess huge passion that you're working to keep bottled up because you're frightened by the intensity you're capable of." He leans in closer. "I know that when we were alone you saw the depth of something so powerful it scared you and sent you scurrying to some emotional cave you imagine keeps you safe." He runs a hand through his hair, making it stand up in tufts, before whispering intimately, "Don't you ever think about that day?"

My heart flaps helplessly for a moment before I'm aware of my family, looking up at us with open curiosity.

I turn to Mom and say, "I'm sorry." As if I cheated on her instead of Jay.

Harley tries to start a slow clap, but Mom gives him a withering look.

"Okay, bro." Harley rises and thumps Pierce on the back. "That's the cue for me to give you a ride home."

Mom nods. "Sure, we'll lift the grounding for you to drive . . . Pierce home."

I refuse to look at him as he thanks Mom and Dad and apologizes for the way things went. Dad says, "No need to be sorry." Which is total crap, because on top of the giant political blowout, Pierce has just tried to ruin Harley's life and accused me of hiding from mine. Very bad dinner guest behavior.

I dart from the table, passing the boys on their way to the door. Thundering unevenly up the stairs, I ignore Pierce when he calls, "Dyna, wait . . ."

As Harley's Jeep pulls out of the driveway, I flop onto my bed and hear Dad through the air vent telling Mom, "I predict we've just met Dyna's first husband."

"Ha!" Mom says. "I don't know why you don't like Jay. He told me in confidence he's thinking of going to Vassar instead of Columbia next year so he can stay close to Dyna."

"What a wuss," Dad grumbles.

I don't have the energy to shout down that I can hear them. Their discussion continues as if we live in a culture where they have some sort of say about my love life. *Thank God we don't.*

"Dyna's been through a lot and has gotten used to Jay being around," Dad says. "I just hope she doesn't mistake that for true love."

"Well, Pierce scares me," Mom says, then after a pause she gives a strange giggle.

"Don't you remember I scared you when we first met?" Dad's voice is deep. *Ugh*, I try not to imagine them kissing. Downstairs goes quiet and I put my pillow over my head.

I can't believe Pierce brought up that day in front of my whole family. We were supposed to pretend that kiss never happened. I turn over and stare at my smooth ceiling until I hear Harley come back home. "Whoa, guys, get a room!" he says, which sends Dad's laugh booming through the house.

"Pierce is pretty cool, huh?" Harley says. "Wonder what's up with him and Dyna."

I reach over, clamp the pillow over my mouth, and scream into it as loud as I can. It feels so good I do it a few more times before flipping face-first onto my bed.

The discussion downstairs turns to the real possibility of Harley applying to the Air Force Academy, and I can't stand to be in this house one more second.

Feeling around until I locate Jay's poem, I stare at his beautiful words about finding our fit.

I dial his number and as soon as he picks up I tell him where he needs to meet me.

"Really? Are you sure?" he asks.

"Yes. Absolutely."

After a pause he says, "I'll come pick you up."

I glance toward my bedroom door. "No, I'll just meet you there."

"It's almost six-thirty, Dyna. The sun will be setting soon and I don't think you should be driving in the dark your first time out."

"Don't worry. I'm not driving."

21

By the time I reach the clearing my leg is throbbing on account of the molten lava that's flowing through it.

Jay rushes forward the moment I hit the turnoff and catches me as I allow my bike to clatter to the ground. "Ungh!" I groan, and clutch my wrapped ankle as he eases me down to sit in the dirt. I look up at his concerned face as a team of endorphins gets busy putting out the fire in my leg.

"I did it!" I laugh in disbelief. "Oh my god, I didn't think I could. But I did it."

His astonishment hardens to anger. "What the hell, Dyna? When you said you weren't driving I assumed you were getting a lift. What made you think you could ride your bike this far?"

"I know, right?" I'm hit with a wave of giddiness as I turn to the swim hole

and gasp.

It is so changed.

The setting sun has dyed the cliff a shimmering rose, and thick patches of red and yellow leaves are doubled in the water's reflection. The effect should be breathtaking, except it's ruined by a new chain-link fence surrounding the whole area. It looks as if the swim hole has been placed under arrest.

"What the . . . ?" My voice goes small and I hug my knees. "A fence?"

"I can't believe they put it up so quickly." Jay grins at me. "Now nobody else can get hurt."

"Nobody . . ." I can't take my eyes off the silver abomination. "That's not . . ."

"Hey." He moves to embrace me, but I'm a marble statue sitting on the ground. "This is a good thing, Dyna. If they'd done this sooner you never would've fallen." He reaches to push the hair off my face but I deflect his hand. I climb slowly to my feet and limp over to the disgusting fence.

My fingers grip at the chain links and I shake with all my strength. The fence responds with a rattling metallic laugh. "This is awful. And it's all my fault."

"I wouldn't say that," Jay says. "In fact, I feel pretty responsible."

"How are you . . . ?" I've caught my breath from the ride, but I still can't finish my sentences.

Jay smiles proudly. "I wrote a letter to the *New Paltz Times* about what a hazard this place is. Well, *was*. This must be the water company's response." He gestures to the fence as if it's a grand prize I've just won.

I want to slap the rubber grin off his face.

I can't believe it. "Now nobody can enjoy the swim hole."

"This place was a lawsuit waiting to happen, if you ask me."

"Well, who the hell did ask you?" Staring at the hideous silver scar, I accuse, "This is how you want to keep me, isn't it? All fenced in."

The color drains from Jay's face. "I just want you to be safe, Dyna-baby." He wavers on his feet, but I don't hold back.

"There is no such thing as safe, Jay. Anything can happen. I can slip in my bathtub and break my damn neck." Jay tilts his head, as if a new angle may help him understand why I'm suddenly so angry.

I don't like feeling this pissed off. I want to push out the words that everything's fine and that the two of us are still okay. But I need to stop being afraid of my own intensity.

I know what has to happen.

"Jay, I will always love you," I tell him. "God, I *literally* owe you my life . . . but we need to break up."

His eyes narrow in confusion, and I'm reeling over what I've just said. I ache to take it back but I can't. It's the truth.

"B-but I saved you," he sputters as if in shock. "I'm responsible for your life, Dyna."

"No, Jay. You're not," I say firmly. "I am."

He sits down hard on the ground like his legs just gave out. I cringe at how much this hurts. When he finally speaks, his voice is so low I can barely hear him. "Is there somebody else?"

I stammer, "I-I-I . . ." Which is enough of an answer for his shoulders to drop.

"But when? I've been with you practically every second you're not at Ulysses . . ." His head snaps up to look at me. "That *Pierce* guy?" The accusation has an edge and I'm immediately defensive.

"No, we're not together. In fact, he probably hates me right now."

Jay laughs. "Dyna, trust me when I tell you, there's no way that guy could ever hate you. Don't think I never noticed the way he looks at you."

"This really isn't about him, Jay." I crouch down to face him. "This is about us being stuck and needing to break out. When we met, you had your sights set on becoming a writer in New York City. Now I hear you're thinking of staying local? Just to be near me?"

"Your mom told you?"

"No. I overheard her telling my dad."

"I was willing to make a sacrifice because I'm in love with you, Dyna. Can't you see that?"

I stand and step up to the fence. "The two of us have been frozen in time, Jay. I've been locked into what happened here. My fall. Being a victim." I rattle the fence for emphasis. "I need to break out and start living again."

Jay's voice bleeds. "But I love being locked in with you."

"I've loved it, too," I say softly. "I honestly have. But there's a part of me that I lost that day. A wild part. I blamed that wild part for messing up my ankle and almost getting me killed. But I can't bottle it up anymore, Jay. I'm sorry."

I don't know how much he can understand, but after a long moment he furrows his brow and drags himself to his feet. I wait a few beats before sliding into a full-body hug. I could sob for the familiar feel of his embrace.

"We hold each other back," I say. "I need to be free, not sheltered. And you!" I pull away and look up at him. "You are going to be a *great writer* one day. And I will be so proud when I hear about it." My voice cracks.

"Well, the best writers *are* all anguished. You're certainly contributing to that right now." His green eyes find mine. "But, Dyna, can't you see what you're giving up? Are you really willing to risk what we have?"

Risk. The word flows over me and settles in my chest. It frightens me to think of leaving Jay's safe arms.

I grip the sides of his waist and look into his eyes, willing him to really hear my words. "Isn't life about the risks?" His face blurs through my tears.

He exhales loudly and looks up at the rails for a moment before hugging me again.

We stay like that for a time. Knowing that when we leave the swim hole, everything will be different. Again.

When Jay finally asks if he can please drive me home I tell him I want to hang out here alone a bit longer.

"Will you at least have somebody pick you up?"

"That's not your worry. I've got this."

He gives me a defeated smile. I close my eyes as he kisses me goodbye and whispers, "Be well, precious wildflower."

When he turns to go I notice the rosy glow of the fading light has shifted to blue. Even if I rush to leave right this moment I'll be riding home in the dark, but I slump down onto a rock anyway.

The water reflects the growing twilight through the fence.

And I wonder just how deep down

the girl who broke that surface can be.

The sun dips below the mountains as I point my bike toward home and start pedaling. I'm trying to make my good leg do most of the work, but every part of me throbs as I maneuver down the trail. The stars are all hiding and I've been indoors for so long I don't even know what phase the moon is in.

A slash of blackness swipes at me and I give a girly scream before realizing it's only a bat. *Pull it together, Dyna.*

As the light fades I can't anticipate the bumps and dips and creatures moving freely in the night. I skid to a stop and root through my bike pack for my headlamp. Thankfully, the batteries still have a little juice, but the beam is just a dim circle of light shaking along the ground in front of me as I push on.

I'm sweating despite the chilly night air. Physically and emotionally shot. Something *huge* crashes through the woods toward me. My headlamp slides askew as I

skid on the fallen leaves.

Barely avoid the deer I've spooked.

The light from my headlamp blinks and goes dark.

Damn batteries.

I stop my bike and fling my head back,

looking up into the black. Hopeless.

And then.

I can't see anything.

But I know they're there.

The undersides of trees.

The sky.

The stars.

I am not alone.

What was that Pierce said in his bedroom? *You can't let any-thing keep you from what you love.*

I walk my bike forward.

Fear has been keeping me from my woods.

Keeping me from what I love.

My eyes adjust to the darkness and I push off again.

Forcing my pedals around, I build momentum. Churn my suffering legs. Turn on Dyna's porno sound track. Dig in and press on endlessly until

the trees break and the moon finally makes an appearance.

Wooden planks rumble beneath my tires and with

a vibrating *woosh*

I glide across the bridge,

surrender to the brilliant river,

and welcome my release.

22

I borrow Harley's Wrangler the next day and drive myself to Ulysses. Mom tried to object, but Dad stepped in and the two of them were brawling sweetly when I left. I can't believe I didn't push myself to drive much sooner. How did I forget how great it feels to just hit the gas and *go*?

The sky looks menacing as I make the turn into the center. My ankle is stiff and sore and I had to wrap it extra-tight, but I'm so happy I don't care. With work, I'm going to do all of the things that I love. I'm excited to tell Pierce about my incredible ride home last night.

When I'd finally parked my bike in the garage and walked through the door, Mom was so mad I didn't have the heart to tell her I'd just broken up with Jay. I tried explaining how significant it was for me to be out on the trail again, but she just gathered her robe tight and stormed off to bed.

Dad stood there for a long moment with his arms crossed. Finally, a smile pulled at the sides of his mouth and he reached out to put his arm around me. The one that has my name tattooed on it. He leaned in to give me a kiss on my forehead and whispered, "That's my girl." I'd smiled at how right he was.

I expect the group to be inside because of the gathering storm, but when I pull up to Ulysses everyone's standing in the parking lot watching the van. Miss is in the driver's seat talking to Sparky.

When I ask what's going on Polly turns toward me and I gasp. Her patch is gone and in place of her ruined eye is a diamond-encrusted glass one.

"Oh my god, that looks fantastic," I say, and I'm not kidding. She looks amazing, like a crazy-beautiful Asian cyborg or something.

Polly flashes a quick smile. "I needed a change."

Frank explains that we're going on a field trip to hike on the mountain in the rain. "Miss decided the lightning storm forecasted this morning will be perfect for Sparky's recovery challenge."

"Wha—?"

Rita nods nervously.

"It's a one-day-only sale on cray-cray," Polly says sarcastically.

I look through the van window at the stress on Sparky's face and feel instant pity. I may be working through my own stuff, but I still think fear of lightning can be a healthy thing.

"This is insane," I say to nobody, and everybody nods in agreement. Everybody besides Pierce, that is. He's sitting on the steps to the deck, scowling at a patch of crabgrass as if it isn't living up to its full potential.

He watches me use my cane to lower myself beside him and then goes back to glaring at the ground.

"You need to talk to her." I gesture to Miss, who has started loading water bottles into the van. "We can't go to the mountain today. The air is filled with electricity. Poor Sparky is terrified."

"Says the girl who's afraid to risk anything." Pierce's eyes are brewing with hostility.

"What the hell's your problem?" I squint at him. "I'm the one who should be pissed after you basically outed our kiss to my whole family."

"*Your* kiss," he says. "You kissed me, remember?"

"Forget it." I rise to leave but he grabs my arm.

"Wait, Dyna . . ." I sit back down and he lets out a sigh. "I'm sorry for the way I acted in front of your parents."

"Well, my dad thinks you're kind of great, actually. But my mom might need some convincing that you don't have a master plan to ruin my life."

"Yeah, I got that impression from her when I called last night."

"You called?"

"I wanted to talk to you, to apologize. But don't worry, your mom made it perfectly clear you ran right out to meet your *boyfriend* the second I left."

I imagine the tone Mom must've used. I'm sure she made it obvious that Pierce's call was not welcome.

"It wasn't like that . . ."

Pierce holds a finger up to my lips and gives a sneer. "I get it, Dyna. We can just go back to pretending nothing ever happened. I guess I was wrong about you all along."

I try to grab his arm as he stands up, but he pulls away.

"Pile in!" Miss hollers, and Pierce is gone before I can even begin to explain. *Damn, he's quick for a one-legged boy.*

By the time I reach the van, Sparky and Pierce are tucked in the way back already. I hear Pierce saying, "Just stay close to me. Who knows? Maybe my metal leg will draw the lightning and keep you safe."

Sparky is too busy gripping the seat in front of him to appreciate Pierce's attempt at humor.

"Buckle up, gang," Miss calls. "I need to hurry if we want the best odds of catching that storm."

I jump into the passenger seat beside her and in a low voice accuse, "Sparky is statistically *more* likely to be struck by lightning again. Not less."

"Says who?" Miss hisses back.

I squint at her. "Do you not have access to the Internet? I looked it up."

"Pshaw," she says as she starts up the van. "You can't believe everything you read on the Internet, Dyna."

"I know that butterfly story of yours is bullshit." She raises her eyebrows and I add, "Ulysses are only found in Australia and I notice you don't have an Australian accent, mate."

She rubs her pendant with her fingers. "Do you honestly think the species of the butterfly is what's important?"

"Um, yes, I do," I say. "Your center is one big sham, starting with the name."

Miss shifts her whole body toward me. "I am running one of the most successful and respected therapy programs in the Mid-Hudson Valley." Her words are emphasized with actual spittle. "Now you can either buckle up or get the hell out, Dyna."

I turn and look at the group of people sitting behind us, watching. Everything in me wants to bail on this trip, but as I absorb each expectant face I know I can't ditch them again. With a growl I turn around, pull my seat belt on, and click myself in.

23

Only batshit-crazy fools would be on the mountain today.

"Park's all ours," Miss announces as she pulls into the empty parking lot. *Yup, batshit-crazy fools.*

Pierce has Sparky totally pumped by now, and the two of them burst out of the van's side door with a roar. They head for the trail leading up the mountain like a two-man stampede.

I tell Miss, "This is a bad idea," but she just ignores me as she helps Rita out of the van.

If I have any hope of talking to Pierce, it looks like I'll have to catch him first. He and Sparky jog down the path, and despite the pain and stiffness from my late-night bike ride, I take off after them. My tightly wrapped ankle hurts like hell and my calf muscle feels like a steel rod as I lurch along, leaning heavily on my cane.

As soon as the boys reach the first bend in the path the trees swallow them whole.

"You guys mind waiting up?" I holler.

"You mind keeping up?" Pierce pokes his head back into view before disappearing again.

An echoing thunder rumbles its warning. Grunting in frustration, I stride faster.

I breathe in the melody of sharp pine and musty birch, and despite everything I feel my insides shifting at being on the mountain after all this time.

I'm back.

The rest of the group begins to fall farther behind as I chase after Pierce and Sparky. I hear Miss tell Polly to "keep it moving, Miss Bling."

I finally catch up at the first overlook. The boys are completely absorbed, staring at the exploding color surrounding the lake below. As well as the dark menacing clouds swarming over it. We are speechless.

The others join us one by one as fat droplets of rain start to fall.

"A heads-up that we were going to be playing outside today might have been nice," Polly shouts. "I would've at least brought an umbrella."

"Sure, your own personal lightning rod." Sparky grins down at her and she elbows him. I hope he gathers the courage to ask her out because I don't believe for a second she's given up on looking for love.

"Whoa," Frank says at the crack of a loud thunderclap. I feel a charge of excitement flow through the group.

"Perfect conditions for facing that struggle, Sparky," Miss announces.

I move toward Pierce just as the sky gives out and releases all the rain it's been holding back. It pours fast and hard, obliterating the view.

Rita pulls her hood up and Polly screams at the liquid on-slaught. Sparky puts an arm around each of them.

For a moment I clutch my arms across my chest, trying to hang on to partial dryness, but it doesn't last long. The rain seeps through my clothes all the way to my skin. I pull my sweatshirt closer and look down at thin canvas shoes that should be hiking boots. I swish them around in the puddle quickly forming at my feet. After a moment, even my Ace bandage is saturated with the cold water.

My annoyance yields to the absurdity of how drenched I am. Utterly soaked. I lift my face to the sky and laugh. *I am on my mountain*. Rita smiles at me and I know she gets it. I am completely present in this moment. I stretch out my arms and give a twirl for good measure.

Miss starts shimmying her hips like that's what they're made for, and Sparky puts his hands over his mouth and gets a beat-box riff going. Rita begins headbanging so hard her braids fling rainwater as they fly up and down, and Frank launches into an awkward running-man dance that is the funniest thing I've ever seen.

Polly slicks her hair back and pauses a moment with both hands behind her head and her elbows sticking out. A smile spreads across her face and she busts a move, flapping her elbows wildly back and forth in time with her pelvis. Sparky starts laughing so hard his beat gets all messed up and Rita squeals with joy.

It's an impromptu dance party in the middle of a thunder-storm on the side of a mountain.

And it is the most fun any therapy group could ever have.

Blurred through the rain I see Pierce watching me. I'm an awkward dancer, but what I lack in skill and rhythm I make up for with zeal. His eyes penetrate me through the rain. Jokingly I give a shoulder shake in his direction. His face hardens and he turns to grab Sparky's arm, calling, "Come on!" over the sound of the rain.

Sparky looks surprised but follows him anyway. They start jogging up the path and the rest of us are forced to follow. Miss and Rita struggle to keep up, but Polly and Frank fall even farther behind. I'm pushing myself to catch them, but Pierce is a strong runner even without his jogging prosthetic.

He clearly wants to get away from me and is dragging poor Sparky along with him. The heavy sheets of rain finally ease up a little and I'm able to see more clearly as I plod down the muddy trail.

When I catch up again, Pierce and Sparky have climbed to an overhang about twenty feet above my head. They're both waving their arms in a wild show of victory and giving manly *Yeahs!* and *Hoo-Ahs!*

Miss and Rita catch up and stand beside me, watching them.

"Hey, guys?" I call. "You do know lightning loves elevation, right?"

Sparky gestures to the mountain rising up behind them. "I was all the way up there when I got hit."

I look at Miss. "Don't even *think* about it."

Polly and Frank move in behind us and Miss announces, "You've done it, gentlemen. This is the pinnacle moment of this journey. Congratulations, Sparky. You've conquered your struggle!" The rain gets heavier again, as if it's applauding with the rest of us.

Pierce and Sparky start doing muscleman poses, shaking their wet hair and making the rest of us laugh.

Frank calls out in a wrestling announcer's voice, "Man. Versus. Thunderstorm!"

There's a terrifying flash of light and

Zttt-Crash!

We're inside the thunder clap.

I try to see in every direction at once.

CrankinShitFrack to the power of nine.

Where the hell did that hit?

Is everyone okay?

The sound of the crash echoes through the valley and continues ringing in my ears. The air crackles with energy.

"Let's get out of here," Sparky shouts, and Frank calls, "Race everyone to the van!"

Nobody argues as the soggy group turns and runs at their various speeds. Miss looks genuinely frightened and is just elbows, ass, and heels as she heads down the trail. I want to shout after her, "I told you so!"

Frank grabs Rita by the hand to help her along the path, and Sparky scrambles down the steep embankment and tucks Polly protectively under one of his big burned arms. When I see the grateful way she looks at him as he guides her toward safety, I think Sparky may have just conquered two mountains in one day.

A shot of terror burns

through me as I realize Pierce

hasn't come down.

With all the rain and confusion I'm the only one to notice. Everyone else is gone.

I move so fast it's as if I never injured my leg at all. Dropping my cane I grab onto the rocks and start pulling myself up.

The climb would be easier if I could use both of my feet and if maybe the rain wasn't pouring down on my head so hard I can barely see. But I know I can do this. I'm practically numb as my arms and leg claw and slide. I make progress and then find myself helplessly skidding back down to start over.

I need to get to Pierce.

It is pure willpower that finally pulls me to the top. My muscles shriek as I drag myself up over the edge.

Pierce. His name forms in my mouth and I hesitate a moment before it escapes in a thin question. "Pierce?" He's clutching the wet ground on his hands and knees. I can see he's breathing heavily but I can't tell if he's been struck or not.

He looks up, streams of water running over his face. His blue eyes are wild. He shifts back so he's kneeling unevenly and crosses his arms in an *X* in front of his chest. His left hand cradles the bandages on his right shoulder where my dad branded him with his buddies' names. And with wings that run with sand.

The lightning crash must've thrown him into some form of shock. I automatically lunge to him.

He flinches away and I stop.

Feeling helpless, I put my hands on my head and wait for him to speak.

Finally I prod, "Maybe we've all had enough therapy for one day."

He looks at me like he doesn't know who I am.

I slump to the ground beside him but he backs farther away, shifting to a sitting position. He keeps one hand on his shoulder as he wipes his wet face with the other.

"You know." I grasp for something to say. Something that will get him to connect back to the present. Connect back to me. "You had a huge impact on my brother. He's already researching the Air Force Academy." It's true. I haven't seen Harley this excited since he first discovered skydiving. Pierce doesn't respond and I put my hand on his arm. He doesn't move away this time. "Pierce, you got my brother to think about his future and swear off smoking pot for good. I know you hate to hear it, but you honestly are a damn hero."

Grunting, he finally lets go of his shoulder but continues staring straight ahead. We sit together, bearing the rain.

Pierce takes another swipe at his face and finally speaks. "My uncle was one of the victims killed in Tower One. From the time I was a little kid I couldn't wait to join the military." He looks at his hands. "Now the things that kept me alive over there, always pushing harder, being quick to react . . . they're not so useful anymore."

"I don't know. Hitting the dirt before getting struck by lightning was a pretty good trick, I think."

He stares at me a moment as if he's trying to decide something. "Why don't you go ahead back to the van. Tell Miss I got a little taken over by events and need a few minutes."

"I'm staying with you." I don't have everything figured out, but I do know where I belong right now. Here. On this mountain. Beside Pierce.

He starts to say something, then shrugs and shakes the water off his head like he's a swimmer just breaking the surface.

The rain has lightened up a little, but the air stays heavy as the two of us sit looking out over the wet, vibrant valley. Thunder rumbles like a growling dog that refuses to leave. I resist the urge to move closer to Pierce as I bite back words that aren't enough.

I reach up to wring out my hair.

He sighs. "I think you were maybe right to quit before. It's probably time for me to take a break from Ulysses."

"What, and miss out on these fabulous field trips?" I flick my fingertips at his face and he flinches at the spray of water that hits him.

"I don't know what made Miss think I was recovered enough to help other people." He glances at me, and I'm stunned once again by the blue of his eyes. "Time to move on before I get somebody killed."

"This wasn't your fault . . ."

"I was acting stupid." He shakes his head. "Trying to prove . . . I don't know what. I just need to accept that I'll never be completely better. I left a piece of myself over there in that desert."

"Uh, *literally*." I knock on his fake leg. He looks at me in astonishment. "What?" I say. "It's okay for you to joke but I can't?"

He goes on. "Everything just seems so pointless. When I was over there things made sense in a way. I just had to stay alive and make sure my brothers on my right and on my left survived. Now, I can't get past the guys who will never make it home." He pulls back the neck of his T-shirt and peels the soaked gauze off his shoulder, revealing his tattoo. I'm taken by the beauty of my father's artwork. Strong wings covered in sand. Even marred by red irritation, it's clear the piece is special.

"I guess you need to live that much harder," I say. "You're doing it for them, too."

"Yeah, I know. I see Rita squeezing a minute out of every second," he says. "I'm just tired, you know? I'm done pushing myself so hard." The fight is drained out of him.

It rises up in me.

The thunder snarls.

I want to prove to him that he didn't die back there in all that sand.

I need him to know that he's alive.

That we both are.

"So what? Now you'll just roll over and quit?" I yell above the storm. His eyes focus on me but my voice doesn't falter. "You think I'll sit here and listen to you talk about giving up after how hard you've pushed me?"

The rain streams down his face as the lines of tension turn to a wave of amusement. He says, "So now you're going to save me?"

"Damn straight." I hold in my smile but feel it reaching my eyes.

He tilts his head. "And how're you planning to do that, Dyna?"

I swipe the water off my face with both hands. "Oh, I am going to be *all over* your ass. No mercy."

He laughs. "And just what will your perfect two-legged boyfriend have to say about all this merciless ass-covering that's about to happen?"

"Who, him?" I shrug. "Things didn't work out."

I have his full attention now and see his Adam's apple jump as he swallows.

"No?" he asks softly. "Why not?"

"Because." My voice is unsteady but my gaze is firm. "He isn't you."

Pierce's chest rises with a deep breath as his eyes stay with me.

After a moment he asks, "Do you remember the story of the tin soldier?"

"Um . . . not really." This isn't the reaction I expected and I'm filled with the weird feeling he's about to reject me.

"Well, you see, there's this tin soldier and he only has one leg. Sound familiar?" He gives the slightest smile and my insides dip. "But he's sturdy and strong and has a big heart, you know?"

I have no idea where Pierce is going with this, but I reposition away in case it's bad.

"So, one day this soldier sees a ballerina doll who has one leg up in the air where he can't see it. Right away he thinks she's perfect for him because she's got only one leg, too."

"So you're looking for a one-legged dancer? Because I can dance way better than I did back there in the rain . . ."

"Will you let me tell this, please?" he says. "And the doll has two legs. He only *thinks* she has one."

I press my lips together.

"So anyway, he knows from the moment he sees her that she's the one for him. And everything he goes through for the whole story is all about getting together with this girl he's in love with." He looks at me for a deep moment.

"Does he?" I practically croak.

"Well." He rubs his hands together and squints. "They kind of end up burning in a fire together, and they melt into the shape of a tin heart."

"Okay . . . that's sad but sort of crazy romantic."

"I've known it since that first day we met. When you lost it on Miss about wanting your mountain. Dyna." He takes a breath. "It's all been about you."

Moving more smoothly than most guys could with two good legs, he closes the space between us and cups my face in one hand. Our eyes are locked for just a beat before I close mine. His hold is gentle but powerful as he pulls my lips to his.

There is nothing safe about this kiss.

This is a kiss made of flood

and fire

and lightning.

This feels so good.

I never want to stop.

His mouth is warm and my arms instinctively wrap around his back to pull him closer. I feel his muscles underneath his soaked T-shirt. They aren't muscles developed on some machine. They were built through endurance and hardship.

Strength born of pain, and I feel that same strength in myself.

We pull apart and the happiness and disbelief on Pierce's face make me laugh.

"What?" he asks, tipping his head to one side.

"Nothing," I say. "Just . . . I can't believe you almost got struck by lightning!"

"Oh, I got struck all right." He slides his hand to the back of my neck and
kisses me with such heat
the rain stops falling.
And the two of us
melt together.

24

She stood on tiptoe, with her legs stretched out, as firmly as he did on his one leg. He never took his eyes from her for even a moment. She was as firm as himself.

Hans Christian Andersen
"The Steadfast Tin Soldier"

"And this one is for Sparky," Miss says. "Congratulations."

She's handing out iridescent blue certificates for our final session out on the deck at Ulysses. We're all wearing jackets, and I clap my cold hands with the others as she presents Sparky with his award certificate. I look at her empty lap and realize there isn't going to be one for me.

"Hey, I know I missed some sessions," I say, "but I thought meeting with you separately made up for that."

During my private sessions with Miss I'd opened up to her about the ways I'd been allowing fear to hold me back. She'd listened thoughtfully as I described my accident in harrowing detail. "There's no going back to ignoring mortality after an experience like that," I said. "But I've finally come to see that being filled with fear is a nasty prank. It blocks us from truly living."

Miss smiled at me and I said, "What?"

"Nothing. Just that I love watching one of my butterflies take flight."

"Let me guess," I said. "We're all *Ulysses* butterflies?"

"Technically, Karners. You were right." The two of us burst out laughing together and she admitted, "I guess I misidentified my butterfly in an encyclopedia when I was a girl and never thought to recheck it. But would you honestly want to go to a place called the *Karner* Center?"

I nodded my head and told her, "If it was here, I just might."

A breeze blows now, and I shiver as Miss says, "I'm sorry, Dyna, but you can't get a certificate. You never completed a recovery assignment."

"You never assigned me one." *I want one of those damn certificates.*

"I was in the process of making arrangements when you disappeared for that—"

"I'm sorry, okay?" I interrupt. "But does it have to be too late?" I look around the circle. "Would you guys be willing to come back to do a challenge with me?"

"You know we'll be happy to," Frank says, and the rest of the group agrees.

"Okay." Miss smiles. "It probably can't happen until the spring, and the mountain has been done already, but I do have a really good idea."

I look at Pierce. "Should I be worried?"

He nods. "Oh yes. You most certainly should."

I'm glad the group has a concrete reason to get back together, and I clap with the rest of them as Pierce shares his plans to become a therapist. "I'm thinking I can help other veterans make the transition back home," he says. "Plus, you know, maybe figure out some of my own junk."

"Tell me about it." Miss chuckles. "I think most of us go into psychotherapy to work through our own issues." That gets everyone laughing.

Pierce is going to make an amazing counselor. Talking with him already helped me decide to go back to school for the rest of my senior year. To be honest, if Mom and I had stuck with our DIY education plan I probably would've finished high school sometime in my mid- to late-twenties.

When she and I stopped by school to reregister me for classes, we ran into Jay in the hallway. He blinked a lot and tried too hard and managed to coat me with guilt, but I'm convinced the right girl is out there for him. Maybe some psycho chick who actually does need to be kept safe.

After spending so much time with Pierce and Rita and the gang, I'm not looking forward to the bullshit pettiness that is universal to the high school experience. But hey, I've just got another eight months to endure. I think I can stand it. Besides, Pierce and I are already planning our trip to hike the Appalachian Trail together after I graduate.

Miss announces we'll be finishing up by revisiting the one-word descriptions we each gave ourselves on our first day.

"So, Dyna, you used the words 'fine' and 'okay,'" she says. "What do you think now?"

I say, "Um, I wasn't fine *or* okay that day."

Polly says, "Yeah, we remember."

We laugh and Miss asks me what I choose as my word today. I allow my eyes to land on Pierce. We smile at each other and I say, " 'Awake.' Today my word would be 'awake.'"

"Good," Miss says.

"Can I get my certificate now?" I ask and she laughs.

Frank is next and his "unemployed" has now become "purposeful." He did such a great job on his "Don't Text and Drive" talk that he's managed to book a number of gigs and is hitting the road. "I can't believe how rewarding it is to talk to teenagers," he says, grinning at me. "They're like these funny, awkward creatures that I enjoy being around."

Sparky is still "Sparky," of course, but he's also "budding" now that he's been able to help harvest the fall vegetables on his farm. Polly looks over at him and twirls the sunflower he brought her today. They smile at each other, and it's clear Sparky's not the only thing in the sharing circle that's budding.

Polly says, "I still have my anger issues . . ."

Rita nods, holding up the sign of the horns, and we laugh.

Polly gives Rita a look of affection and goes on. "But now I know how I deserve to be treated. So, instead of being 'pissed' over what brought me here, I guess I'd have to call myself mostly 'blessed' today."

Rita proclaims she's now "*abundantly* blessed" for getting to know all of us before she departs. She tells us about a type of moth that emerges from its cocoon with no mouth parts for drinking nectar. "From the moment it gets its wings that moth begins to starve to death. But just think of all those caterpillars who never even get to fly." She tips her face upward. "Oh. That moth," she says. "It makes it all the way into the *sky*!"

Rita's heartbreaking moth makes me think of Alexander Supertramp. He may have starved to death, but at least he made it into the wild.

Looking around at my beautiful patched-together group of broken, hopeful people, I realize—his fatal mistake was going alone.

EPILOGUE

"Three . . . Two . . . One!"

"Eeeeeee!" I scream as I plummet through the air.

My big brother is strapped to my back and a parachute is strapped to his. I just stepped out of an airplane and I'm a bit preoccupied with the falling sensation that is really more of an *overwhelming full-body experience* than a simple sensation. I can't breathe as the wind batters my face and roars in my ears.

"Keep your eyes open," Harley instructs calmly behind me. "Embrace every second."

".I'm trying," I call. "I'm just freaking out!"

He laughs. "Don't make me embarrassed to say we're related. Your friends are handling this better than you are."

I stretch my neck as far back as I can and look above us through the enormous goggles I'm wearing.

Sure enough, there's Pierce strapped to his tandem jumper, arms outstretched with one leg of his flight suit pinned back. He shouts a loud "Hell, yeah!" and waves at me with the hugest grin ever. I whimper in response.

Above Pierce, so small I can barely make them out, are Frank and Miss with their guides. I recognize Rita's ringing call to "rock on!" from the plane. She's amazing her doctors, hanging in to see spring unfurl.

Just like she promised.

"It's the way I want to remember this world," she says as she keeps right on living. Loving her is a huge risk, knowing the empty place she will leave.

But I do not hold back

or protect myself.

I love that old lady like crazy.

Just like the rest of my mismatched gang of supporters. Polly and Sparky opted to keep their feet on the ground for this one, and Miss is just fine with that. It seems her radical pursuit of the Struggle has been tempered a bit by nearly getting her entire therapy group electrocuted. Then again, skydiving as a rule should probably always be optional.

My parents are down on the ground, too, watching us with their motorcycles parked nearby. We're still getting used to the news that Harley got into the Air Force Academy. He leaves for Colorado in a few months and it's a huge challenge to trust that he'll be safe, but I'm learning to have faith. *Besides,* I look at the landing field far below us, *it's not as if his life was ever risk-free.*

My lower leg tingles, reminding me of the awesome tat I got from Dad last week. He highlighted my scar to look like a tree branch surrounded by bright blue butterflies that are so detailed you'd swear they can fly. Written in a swirl along the branch is my own version of the family motto:

The greatest risk of all . . . is taken with the heart.

I glance back toward Pierce. Being in love with him
is so scary.
But he's worth the risk.
The two of us push each other to go deeper, farther, higher,
and he tells me every day
how remarkable I am.
And you know what?
He's right.   *I kind of am.*
Adrenaline stings my tongue as I look out at the widest view
I've ever experienced. My mountains stand watching, unmoving,
and I give myself over to the fall. Trust that the chute will be
there when we need it.
My wide-stretched arms embrace the whole world.
I'm connected to nothing and everything all at once.
I breathe sky now.
I am not afraid.
I am alive and I am soaring.
Free.
Pierce gives a hearty "Hoo-Ah!"
and my laughter punches the air.
"That's it." Harley senses the shift in me. "There's that Dy-
namite."
Yes,
here I am.

ACKNOWLEDGMENTS

To the incredible Margaret Ferguson, Ammi-Joan Paquette, Susan Dobinick, and the teams at FSG and EMLA: thank you for making this amazing journey possible. And to Ben Liotta, James Spadola, Eddie Boyle, and all those veterans who have left pieces of themselves in faraway places: you are beyond remarkable.

Special thanks for help from Dr. Lorri Lankiewicz, Ellen DeMonte, MSN, RN, and the generous clerks at the Haviland-Heidgerd Historical Collection in New Paltz. Any factual errors here are my own. To talented writer folks Alison, Amanda, Michelle[2], Kristin, and Shana, and to my wonderful extended family: the Boyles, Giels, Courtneys, Spadolas, Bateses, Melansons, and Pirros: thank you all for keeping me "on belay."

Always and forever to Trinity and Aidan, who teach me more about love every day: you're both my favorite. And especially to Brett: you rode into my life on a big black Harley and have taken me on the greatest adventure. Thank you for being you.